The author being born close to London's main airport and then spending his formative years in a leafy Hampshire town that is home to a major RAF base may be the reason for his chosen trade. At the age of 66 and now retired from a career of nearly five decades in which time the author travelled the world and spent much of that time on the 'Dark' continent he finally found the time to fulfil his desire to write a novel.

Information gained and stored in his memory of places seen and events witnessed are the basis for this story.

Mark Dawson Conroy

A CALL OF NATURE

AUSTIN MACAULEY PUBLISHERS™

LONDON * CAMBRIDGE * NEW YORK * SHARJAH

A CIP catalogue record for this title is available from the British Library.

ISBN 9781035800230 (Paperback)
ISBN 9781035800247 (ePub e-book)

www.austinmacauley.com

First Published 2023
Austin Macauley Publishers Ltd®
1 Canada Square
Canary Wharf
London
E14 5AA

I would like to thank my daughters Rebecca and Vanessa for their help in the writing of this novel, without their skills this would still be confined to my computer and also to Chantelle for her assistance regarding her native language of 'Afrikaans'. Sentences which I have included in my novel.

Part 1

Chapter 1

It was early November and the dry season still had another month or so to go before the rains would hopefully arrive and turn the dust bowl of hard dry earth and brittle dead grass back into the verdant green it had previously been. It was, for me however, just another sweltering day in the bush and at three thirty in the afternoon, the sun was trying its hardest to make life uncomfortable. We had been working since early morning and would welcome a cool shower and an even cooler beer but that would have to wait.

The team had packed up the drilling rig and put the equipment on the truck and were anxiously waiting for me to complete the sealing of the temporary cap on the pipe before we could set up camp for the night.

If we were too far away from the 'B' team as we called them, we would make camp at our location otherwise we would camp as one unit and share resources but in this case, they were several hours drive away so we would make camp somewhere close to the village.

Our job was to drill the borehole(s) at the required location and cap off the supply and then move on to the next drilling site, theirs was to install the plumbing and pump system; the system worked well, with them following our efforts within a few days but we had heard that there were a few delays in the supplies that they required, so the villagers might have to wait a bit longer for their supply.

The borehole had brought forth a bountiful supply of good clean water, more than enough to keep the villagers and their animals happy.

Nature made a call which required my immediate attention before I cleared up for the day and so picking up my trusty rucksack that contained everything that I might need in a hurry and never left my side, I headed for a quiet spot away from the village to attend to my needs. I had dutifully covered my gift to Mother Nature with some earth and was carefully leaving the thicket of thorn bush when I heard the sound of several vehicles approaching at high speed.

At first, I thought maybe it was more supplies for the medical team that had arrived late that morning but the noise seemed to be coming from several directions, not just the dirt road that we had used.

I stopped in my tracks at the sound of screams emanating from the village, shortly followed by gunfire.

I carefully retreated to my hole in the thicket, I convinced myself it wasn't cowardice; I was in no doubt given the cries of terror and the staccato of automatic gunfire that if I showed myself, I would not leave this place alive. Better to lay low until the madness ceased and the militia moved on, then come out, look for survivors and try to get to safety and let others know of the atrocity.

The noise was horrific, from my concealed space I could see the outskirts of the village and every so often a villager would make a break for freedom, only to be either shot or if it was a young woman, to be chased, caught and dragged back screaming, often being beaten and kicked as they went.

The hut nearest to me appeared to be being used for holding some of these woman, I soon realised why. Men would enter, woman would scream, cry in pain and then be thrown sobbing out into the dust, naked or clothed in tatters to crawl away if they could, before being murdered with a bullet or two. This continued whilst gunfire still rang around the village. It was sickening! But to try and help would be certain death and given what I had witnessed so far, it would probably be a most uncomfortable death.

As I lay amongst the dead leaves and broken twigs, my senses were alerted by movement in front of and to the right side of me, a goat making a break for freedom chased by two youths, one holding a rifle, was heading my way. I froze in horror, not daring to move, hardly taking a breath.

The youths paused their pursuit, the armed one lifted the rifle butt to his shoulder and took aim. The goat stumbled and cartwheeled into the dust, the sound of the gunshot reaching my ears as it did so.

It lay not more than fifteen metres from where I was hidden; my heart pounding loudly within my chest, I waited for the inevitable.

Whooping with delight, the youths sauntered towards their prize casually stepping over the bullet-riddled body of a young woman who only a short time earlier had been unceremoniously thrown from the doorway of the nearest hut by her abusers. Torn and bleeding, she had managed to crawl only a short distance before a burst of automatic gunfire from another of the abusers, laughing as he squeezed the trigger and released her from her agony.

Grasping the still quivering body of the goat by its horns and thankfully totally oblivious of my presence, the youths dragged it back to the confines of the village. It would no doubt be in the cooking pot before the day was done.

I felt sick to the pit of my stomach, not with the killing of the goat, that would have happened sooner or later anyway but with the total disregard for the body of the young woman. Life appeared to have little or no meaning to these people, they seemed to be devoid of humanity.

Still lying among the leaves and twigs, I watched as two men dragged what appeared to be a white woman into the hut; she was struggling bravely but no match for the two who had her in an iron grip. The screaming and cursing continued, followed by salacious laughter from the captors. Another obviously senior member of the militia entered the hut. He was a tall, powerfully built bull of a man, with a voice to match.

I heard screams of terror and then pleadings for mercy before the sound of physical violence followed by the distinctive crack of the palm of a hand upon soft flesh repeatedly carried out, accompanied by laughter from her captors. Her resistance caused her more beatings; perhaps, realising the futility of struggling she submitted possibly in a vain attempt to be spared the inhuman treatment.

Loud sobbing interspersed with obscenities came from the young woman while laughter and grunts of pleasure could be heard from those who took turns upon her. Screams of pain followed as the men enjoyed themselves with their captive. This continued for probably fifteen to twenty minutes before several men left the hut laughing as they went, the bull of a man fastening a wide, dark-coloured belt with a pistol holster attached to his waist as he strode away. I heard no more sounds from the hut.

The sound of gunfire had ceased and I could hear what I presumed to be orders being given, it was then that I saw smoke emanating from within the village as hut after hut was being burned to the ground. If I didn't act now, it would be too late. I had to see in that hut.

I eased myself from my hiding place, carefully avoiding the thorns, the last thing I needed to do was stab myself and cry out in pain.

Warily, I crept towards the hut, my recently used trenching tool firmly in my grasp as my one and only weapon. There was no cover, just beaten earth. I heard talking; I froze, not that it would have helped me but no one appeared. I carried on and reached the hut, the acrid smell of burning flesh and cow dung huts was not one that I will ever forget.

A quick look around and I entered the hut, the beaten earth floor was littered with torn clothing, vomit and other bodily fluids. I saw what appeared to be a young white woman lying prone and naked on the floor, her lower body was a bloody mess.

I moved quickly towards her and turned her over, motioning her to keep quiet in case she was still alive and cried out in alarm. She was alive! But appeared to be in a catatonic state, she showed no recognition of my being there. She was staring at the roof, totally oblivious of anything else. I had to move fast if we were to get out of there alive, I could hear the fires and those who caused them getting closer.

It was a struggle to lift her from the floor, she offered no resistance but no help either; thankfully those five months of hole-digging and equipment-lifting in the bush had put some muscle on my puny body.

A fireman's lift completed, stuffing the handle of my weapon through my waistband I peered from the doorway of the hut, not seeing anyone I cautiously emerged carrying my cargo.

Hardly daring to breathe but with approaching darkness and smoke on my side, I moved towards the safety of the bush. We made it. I laid my human cargo on earth, out of sight of the village but close to my thorn-bush thicket in order that I could retrieve my rucksack.

It was from there that I watched as a militiaman carrying a flaming torch appeared at the hut we had just left, my heart missed a beat as I thought to myself, *'If he looks inside all hell will break loose; he didn't, he just touched the torch to the roof and then threw it inside.'*

I moved out of the thorn-bush thicket once more, this time carrying my precious rucksack. The rucksack was the means of our survival, although it didn't contain a means of communication (phones don't work well in the bush) and not having one was less a temptation for a thief; it did contain essentials for life.

The sound of vehicles leaving the village was a welcome distraction. I gave it about thirty minutes then after checking my precious cargo, I decided to make a foray into what was left of the village to see if there were any survivors that I could help and if not, to hopefully find some food.

There was not one survivor to be found, just bodies and remains of partially burned bodies in the remains of the huts, all either very young or older persons, the militia had 'recruited' all those of impressionable age into their 'Murderous cabal'.

Searching among the devastation for food or indeed anything of use, I came across some wound dressings that had been looted from the medical vehicle that had brought the team to the village, then dropped for me fortunately, they went into my rucksack, the medical vehicle like the vehicle that I had arrived in was a burnt-out wreck, my colleagues like the medical staff were all dead.

It was now too dark to see properly, there were obviously no survivors and as it was doubtful that the militia would return to the scene of their crimes, I decided that it would be best to spend the night in what remained of the village.

I returned to pick up my 'cargo' from her place of safety, hoping that she was not only still alive but hopefully able to talk. Alive yes but still in deep shock, I could only hope that being in the village once again would not cause greater trauma.

One of the huts close to where I had been working at the borehole was only semi-destroyed and offered some protection for the night.

It was too dark to attend to the wounds of the as yet unknown woman but it did seem as though the bleeding had stopped; good job too as the last thing I needed was a pack of hyenas turning up hot on the scent of warm blood, although with all the bodies lying around, they would have plenty of choice.

I prepared myself with some stout looking poles just in case and settled down to a fitful nights' sleep.

Chapter 2

An African sunrise is a sight to behold, the sky streaked in a myriad colour but the scene of utter carnage and devastation in the village took the magic away.

Animals had been there in the night making the scene even worse, half-eaten human carcases strewn around with vultures now squabbling over the remains was a truly sickening sight.

Water was my first priority. My trusty rucksack once again came to the rescue; included in the contents was a water bladder which would hold 5 litres, not a lot for two people but better than nothing. I retrieved it from the hut and proceeded to the borehole luckily untouched by the events of the previous afternoon.

Although the borehole was capped off whilst awaiting the installation of the rest of the plumbing, there was a bleed valve that I could open to fill my water bladder; the trouble was it let the water out at an incredible rate and I lost more than was required to fill the bladder.

On returning to the hut, I was surprised to see that the woman who in the light of day appeared to be about thirty years old had moved into the 'foetal' position and pressed up as close as possible to the darkest part of the remaining wall of the hut.

Her eyes, bloodshot and wide open with fear, stared at me through her tangled matted mess of blond hair.

I squatted down about a metre from her and gingerly offered her the water bladder whilst explaining who I was and that I would not hurt her. After what seemed an eternity, she accepted the bladder and began to drink thirstily. I urged her to take it slowly or it would make her sick, she just glared at me but seemed to slow a little.

Eventually, she stopped drinking and placed the bladder on the floor but did not speak, although she seemed to be becoming more aware of her surroundings and of the fact that she was semi-naked.

I picked up the bladder and took a drink myself, then resorting once more to my rucksack, I pulled out two of the energy bars which I often carried with me, especially if I was going somewhere where food could be somewhat questionable and offered one to the woman, who having accepted it, devoured it with gusto.

We sat in silence for a while, more water was drunk and when I produced a shirt from my rucksack and offered it to her, she not only accepted it but she said thank you. The spell had been broken.

I told her my name again and asked her own, "Johanna," she replied.

"Pleased to meet you," I replied adding, "but perhaps it could have been in better circumstances." That elicited a smile but I could see that she was having a hard time taking it in.

Johanna was still naked from the waist down and streaked in dried blood and dirt; without some form of dressing, the area would get infected. It would be very awkward to address the issue but it had to be done.

"Johanna," I said, "are you aware of what happened yesterday?" She looked at me and tears filled her eyes, then she tried to cover her blood-encrusted regions.

"It's OK, I said I will help you through this but you need to get cleaned up and get some kind of covering on. I will get you some more water to wash with and find you something to put on."

She could hardly move; when she tried to stand, it was obviously painful but she managed to wash away some of the dried bloodstains. However, the bleeding started again.

"I have some 'penicillin' pills in my rucksack that you can take to help fight off infection, that's if you are not allergic and some antibiotic cream to put on your wounds," I said to her, "and I have an idea for some clothing in that area, I just hope you are not too fussy."

She looked at me oddly and said that 'penicillin' was fine and the cream would help but she could not be fussy about the clothing.

I explained that if I went 'commando' she could have my underpants! I further explained that I would wash them at the borehole first, so they might be a little damp.

Once again, a smile appeared on her face this time before a widening of her eyes.

"Thank you," she said, "I don't think washing at the borehole will do much and anyway the 'penicillin' should kill any germs."

"I'll give you some privacy to tend to your wounds," I said, "and at the same time, spare you the sight of me going commando."

"I'm a nurse," she said, "I've seen it all before, besides you're doing it for me and I might need some help applying this cream."

"Hardly the height of fashion I'm sure but they will keep me clean," she exclaimed when I returned to the hut holding a pair of sneakers among other objects that I had found amongst the ruins. The pistol that I had found was tucked into my waistband and would be placed into the rucksack at the soonest but without disclosing that I had it. The sneakers were welcomed with special delight as they were actually her own.

"We have to get moving, it's no good staying put; help might not arrive for quite a while and we have not got much food plus with all the corpses around us, the scavengers will arrive in droves and I did not survive one massacre to be part of another," I said to Johanna.

"Can we give it till tomorrow?" she asked, "I don't feel very mobile at the moment and I am sure that HQ will send out a search party because we haven't called in."

"OK," I said, "I had better make our accommodation more secure but at the first sign of trouble, we will have to go."

We waited for the rest of the day, ate another energy bar and drank copious amounts of water, it was clear from the way Jo, as I called her, moved and gasped when she needed to pee that she was in a great deal of pain and that to move on would not be an easy task.

All day long, the scavengers had hung around the village perimeter but it wasn't until nightfall that they felt bold enough to enter for the feast. The sound of the corpses being ripped apart was horrendous and we got very little sleep that night but we dare not light a fire just in case anyone noticed.

The next morning, we made our decision; help had not arrived and we could not stay another night without the risk of becoming part of the feast.

Water bladder refilled, we headed off towards civilisation and safety. It was slow going and especially painful for Jo. She said that every step seemed to tear at her wounds and despite the use of wound dressings stuffed into (my) now her underpants, blood was soon seeping through.

Chapter 3

We followed the compass on a south-easterly heading, which I hoped would bring us to the town of 'Metarica'. I estimated that it would take at least ten days and I hoped that in that time we should be able to catch some food and with a river that I had seen on previous journeys in that area, we would be OK for water.

Shade was the biggest problem, although open grassland would have been the easiest route, it would offer no protection from either the sun or predators (animal or human). We were acutely aware of our predicament and as painful as it might be, it had to be the long way round.

Night-time would be a real problem because the large predators not only hunt at night but can also climb trees and anyway Jo was finding it difficult to walk, let alone climb a tree.

Apart from briefly stopping to take a drink, we trudged slowly but steadily onward, taking advantage of shade whenever possible. We snacked on the last two energy bars while we walked, food would now need to be caught and cooked.

As dusk approached, the need for night-time shelter grew more urgent and we spotted a small rocky outcrop that looked reasonably easy to negotiate, except for someone in Jo's condition but we made it and with a little searching for fuel and a few rocks, I made a fire that would keep us warm and the predators at bay.

That night with our backs to a large boulder and a fire to our front we slept, feeling secure for the first time in two days.

Jo slept fitfully, occasionally lashing out and crying in pain but remembered nothing of it in the morning. I used those wake-up calls to stoke up the fire and at sunrise, the fire was still burning.

Rummaging through my rucksack, I found a tea bag, what a surprise! I poured some of our water into my mess tin (another item from my rucksack) and laid it onto the hot embers. With the water bubbling furiously, I threw in the tea bag, removing the mess tin from the heat and allowing the water to cool a while before attempting to drink the light brown liquid. Ah, hot tea to start the day, pity about the lack of sugar. But we were grateful for small mercies and it started the day off on the right note.

By now, Jo was a mass of purple and yellow bruises mostly in the shape of a human hand but most striking was the complete imprint around the back of her neck where she had been forcibly held face down; I could only guess why.

I extinguished the fire and helping Jo to her still rather shaky feet, we descended the rocky outcrop and made our way towards our destination.

Given Jo's slow but obviously painful pace, we would be lucky to make more than about five miles a day and at that rate, ten days to Metarica was a little optimistic but we plodded on, occasionally stopping briefly for a drink from our diminishing water supply.

The sun was now directly overhead and the sweat on our bodies was drying almost as it appeared, with salt encrustation marks on our clothing growing ever larger.

The unrelenting mosquitoes had been feasting on us during the night and angry red blotches were fighting for space, Jo looked worse than me on this score because of the bruises and scratches from her attackers.

Whatever else happened today, we had to find water. I wasn't too worried about the quality of the water as I had purification tablets and a water purifying hand-pump in my rucksack but we needed water. Food could wait a day or so.

In the near distance, we could see that not only did the land appear to rise but it seemed to be much greener and tree-covered. I thought at first that the heat and dehydration were causing some kind of mirage but I knew that this part of Mozambique has some tropical foliage; this meant that not only were we heading in the right direction but there would be fruit to eat and possibly water trapped in some of the plant leaves. We pushed on, the thought of full bellies and quenched thirst foremost in our minds.

The foliage seemed to be moving ever further from us as we toiled under that hot sun until at last, the ground began to rise and the air seemed to change, the sweat on our bodies no longer dried as before, beads of it were running down our faces.

The greenery was within reach but it looked dense and impenetrable, we walked along the edge of it for some time, looking for some way in when Jo said to me that she could smell smoke. I sniffed and there did appear to be a whiff of it in the air. We almost hurried in the direction that it was coming from, perhaps a village and maybe help, we hoped. As we got closer, we could also smell food being cooked, we were tantalisingly close when a sound rang out that stopped us in our tracks.

We could hear military like commands and the sounds of many feet along with the unmistakeable rattle of rifles being shouldered but what shook us most was the voice that was issuing the commands; the same booming voice that issued the commands at the village we had come from and the same voice that belonged to the man, who along with others had brutally raped and beaten Jo. I caught Jo as she slumped towards the ground, traumatised no doubt by the fact that we had travelled this far only to be possibly confronted by the same sadistic brutes.

I hefted Jo over my shoulder in a fireman's lift and slowly and carefully backtracked, not daring to look back. Eventually, I found what I thought could be a way in to the undergrowth; in our hurry to follow the smoke, we had gone right past it but it would not be an easy task whilst carrying Jo. I gently eased her onto the ground and pulled her into the dense growth as far as I could. The progress that she had made towards normality the past few days had evaporated and she was now once again a quivering wreck.

I let her rest for a while, whilst pondering on our predicament and what to do next. Reaching out and gently touching her arm as so not to alarm her, I said, "Look Jo, we have got to make a move, we can't stay here much longer; it will be dark soon and darker even sooner in the trees, besides there's probably thousands of mosquitoes just waiting for our blood and I'd rather find some protection from them."

She looked at me through wide open but frightened eyes, "But what about them?" she said, meaning the militia.

"Don't worry," I said, "I won't let them take you." And with that I reached into the front pocket of my rucksack and withdrew the pistol, her eyes seemed to open even wider.

"Where did you get that?" she asked. I told her that I had found it during my search of the village the morning after the raid and added that I think it probably belonged to the leader. I noticed that he had a holster on his hip when he left the hut, that's why I didn't light a fire that night in case he came back for it.

"If I ever see him again, I will return it 'sharp-end first'; it's got five rounds left in the clip and one in the breech, any one has his name on it."

I had cleaned the pistol thoroughly the previous evening when Jo was asleep. After working out how to strip it down, I deduced it was a Russian weapon because of the Cyrillic writing on the barrel but other than that I did not know. My only hope was that it still worked, I didn't have enough ammo to test it.

I stuck the pistol in my waistband for easy access, making sure that the safety was on. I offered my hand to Jo to help her to her feet, she readily accepted it; maybe the thought of putting a round into that bastard had galvanised her in some way.

With my rucksack on my back and Jo on her feet, we started to push into the dense undergrowth.

Progress was very slow, we tried as best as we could not to leave a trail but that was not easy in some places, so we just had to hope that no one came along.

As we climbed higher, the trees started to thin a little but it was still tough-going and Jo's wounds had started to bleed again. Darkness was rapidly falling and a place to hide was urgently sought.

Luck was on our side, we saw a lighter area ahead, bathed in the dying light of the sun and to our immense surprise and delight, we found ourselves looking at a semi-circular cliff face about ten metres high. Water flowed from what I can only describe as a mouth-like opening about three metres wide and a metre from the top of the cliff that was cascading down to fill a circular pool.

The denseness of the undergrowth had muffled the sound of the water. The area around the pool was sheer cliff and enclosed for roughly three hundred degrees, leaving only a small area through which the water flowed away into the undergrowth, strangely though there did not seem to be a great deal of water leaving the pool.

We decided to hole up high in the undergrowth to the left of the pool, we figured that if anyone came for water then they would approach from below and from the right as there was less growth; the only worry was that if we moved in our sleep, we would fall over the cliff and take an early bath.

We ate some bananas that we had picked from a bush growing along the path we had taken, drank a little water and tried to make ourselves as mosquito-proof as possible.

Exhaustion took its toll and we were soon asleep, I didn't bother with a fire for obvious reasons.

Chapter 4

Morning found us huddled together and once more, the mosquitoes had feasted on us; there was hardly any space left un-bitten.

The sun had broken through and was throwing its rays onto the opposite side of the pool from us, I could see that nothing had disturbed the area for quite a while; *'Very strange,'* I thought, *'not even any animal tracks!'* However, it was good news for us.

I decided to fill the bladder and purify the water by adding a tablet and whilst the tablet did its work, we could eat.

I said to Jo, "Watch the water in the pool for movement while I fill the bladder and shout if you see anything, I don't fancy getting eaten."

"OK," she said.

I stopped at the pool's edge crouched and leaned forward to immerse the bladder and once again the thought struck me as to how little water was actually running from the pool.

I stood up, looking around. I found what I was looking for, a small broken branch; I walked over, picked it up and went back to the pool, sensing movement above me, I looked up and Jo was shrugging her shoulders with arms outspread as though to say, "What are you doing?"

"Watch," I said and I threw the stick into the pool, it didn't do quite what I expected. I thought that given the small outflow, there was probably an underground exit, there was but instead of the stick coming towards the edge of the pool, it whizzed round and round in the centre then disappeared like going down a plughole.

A whirlpool and quite a strong one at that! No bathing in this pool. This explained the lack of animal tracks, they must be aware of the phenomena. Jo had witnessed it from above and indicated her astonishment, she also told me not to fall in whilst filling the bladder with water.

Bladder filled, I re-joined Jo above the pool and whilst we ate, we expressed our amazement at what we had witnessed.

Jo needed to clean and redress her wounds, bathing in the pool was not on the agenda but she could still carefully wash the areas. The wound dressings that I had salvaged from the village were by this time disintegrating and she would need something to replace them. I had noticed while at the pool some moss that was growing beside the waterfall and I remembered reading an article about some tribe somewhere who used moss as a soft but absorbent padding. I had been thinking of swimming over to edge of the waterfall to try and grab some that was before I discovered the whirlpool.

I accompanied Jo to the edge of the pool and tried my best to give her some privacy while she cleaned herself, I couldn't help but notice her slender toned figure. I had to stay close in case she fell in, she had almost completed her clean-up when we heard a strange almost gurgling sound that seemed to come from the pool itself, the water rippled and the level of water in the pool sank by a few centimetres for just a few seconds before returning to its prior level.

That was weird but what also occurred at the same time was beyond belief; as the water level dropped, a ledge appeared around the left-hand rim of the pool that would allow access to the moss. The ledge disappeared from view as the water level returned to its original height and because the sunlight never pierced that part of the pool, the ledge would not be seen from above.

I decided that as soon as Jo was safely away from the pool's edge, I would attempt to gather some moss. I had about fifteen metres of rope attached to my rucksack, it was one of my finds at the village during my pre-departure forage and I decided that I would tie one end around my waist and the other to a tree close to the pool; if I fell in, I hoped that Jo could pull me to safety.

I spaced a few knots along the rope to give a handhold and with Jo paying out the tied-off rope, I edged my way carefully along the slippery ledge, probing with what I hoped was a strong piece of broken branch as I went. I reached the waterfall's edge and started to gather some moss, I was getting drenched, I moved a little further into the refreshing flow of water and found myself at the entrance of what appeared not only to be a cave but almost certainly a place of refuge.

Little light filtered through the waterfall, so I first tried waving my branch into the recess, I couldn't feel anything so I decided to throw it in as far as I could.

I was at the end of my rope tether and I did not want to risk falling, I threw the branch as hard as I could, it landed some way in as far as I could tell.

Excited, I made my way back to the pool's edge and safety.

"Jo," I said, "I've found somewhere where we can hole up safely for a few days and give your wounds a chance to heal, you're in no fit state to carry on and I cannot carry you but I'm not going to leave you; it might mean a diet of bananas and water though."

I told her what I had found but also that it would need further investigation before moving in, I didn't think it would be inhabited but there was always a chance.

She agreed. I think the travelling had been a cause of concern to her and she would be glad of the rest.

I looked around for another anchorage point for the rope and found one that although gave me the extra length I needed, it meant that Jo would not be able to pull me to safety. Well, nothing ventured, nothing gained.

I tied off the rope to its new anchor point and armed with another stout branch and with my wind-up torch clipped to my waistband, I ventured once more along the ledge, this time I continued straight through the waterfall's edge where I unclipped and turned on my torch. Shining its beam into the blackness revealed a cave of quite large proportions.

I untied my rope tether and wedged it safely into a convenient rock cleft. I ventured forward, my torchlight being swung side to side looking for signs of life or danger, none was found but what I did find was signs of previous human habitation, a little way in from the entrance and concealed behind a rock ledge was a fire hearth and to one side was some very old and very dry wood. Magic! We were moving in.

I could hardly contain my excitement as I made my way back to Jo. We had a few preparations to make and the sooner the better.

Besides ourselves, we needed to carry in some food, whatever we could pick from nearby without making it obvious that people were around. Jo had shown me how monkeys gather fruits and so we tried to mimic that in case anyone came along. Then we needed wood for the fire, there was plenty lying around but most was damp and once again, we did not want to leave a trail. We decided to take small amounts from different areas so as not to make it obvious.

Getting it into the cave would be another matter, several trips with a full rucksack was doable but not easy; balance was key and thank goodness for the rope.

Firewood was definitely the hardest task, under normal circumstances we would have floated it across the pool but the whirlpool put pay to that idea. We managed it by tying the wood in a bundle and carefully and precariously dragging it around the very edge of the pool close to the ledge, of course it was very wet but it would dry.

It was a team effort for sure but we made It and we could sleep soundly and safely for the first time in days.

We had the fire lit within a few minutes of taking residence, firewood courtesy of the previous inhabitant. I stood in the entrance of the cave with my back to the waterfall and you could not see the fire, not even a glow on the cave walls.

As the last of sun's rays disappeared and darkness fell, we could no longer see the fall of water but the sound was strangely hypnotic and soothing. With the fire burning and once again our bellies full of bananas and some other fruit that Jo had found, we fell into a deep satisfying sleep. Only once that I recall did Jo stir in the night.

The morning light made the curtain of water shine like silver, the fire was soon burning brightly and I put the mess tin on a hot stone surrounding the dancing flames to boil, it wasn't for tea but to give Jo some sterilised water with which to wash her wounds. Her facial and body wounds were healing quite well but those of a more intimate nature were swollen and presumably infected and had been bleeding frequently during our journey.

The wound dressings salvaged from the village were washed the day before at the poolside but the wadding part of them had totally disintegrated. I hoped that the moss from the rock face would take its place. That too would be placed in the boiling water for sterilisation prior to use.

Now that morning had come and with the extra light of the fire, we could see more of our surroundings. We still needed the torch for the deeper recesses, the cave was much larger than first thought; exploring could wait.

Jo washed carefully whilst standing naked in the mouth of the cave, the falling water running in rivulets down her body taking with it the grime and stains of the past days; her hair was also relieved of the accumulated dust and grime, her skin positively glowing from the shock of the cold water, her bruises and wounds in stark contrast to her lightly bronzed skin-tone.

My turn next, we would watch for each other during this process over the next few days, we hoped that we wouldn't have company but we needed to be alert just in case.

Oh, what a feeling, the cool water running over my dirty sweat-stained body, no soap but this was as good as it gets. Body washed, the clothes that we had were next and then we dried them on a pole near the fire.

"Martin," that was the first time that she had called my name, "I need some help!"

"Sure," I replied, "what can I do?"

"It's a bit delicate," she said, "can you look at my wounds, down there?" she added, "I can't see what they look like and I don't want to use the antibiotic cream if it's not needed."

"Blimey!" I said, "That's a first, yes of course, but give me a few minutes to wind up the torch for a good light."

Jo was a nurse, so I suppose this was no big deal for her but for me it was. However, it needed to be done, Jo needed to be fit if we were going to be able to get back to civilisation.

She laid back and slowly and painfully parted her legs, exposing herself to me, the damage done to her was extensive and obviously extremely sore. I explained to her as best I could and guided her fingers to the parts that I was talking about. She asked me to apply the cream to the areas as gently as possible, which I did as carefully and gently as I could but it still elicited gasps of pain in some places.

I noticed also that fresh blood was staining below the area that I was attending to and so, I suggested that she should turn over and let me see from where it was emanating. She duly obeyed, she was torn in her anal region, hence the bruising to the back of her neck. The wound, although raw and bleeding, looked infection free but I applied some cream anyway.

"Right," I said, "let's get you dressed." I placed some of the (hopefully) sterilised moss into the wound dressing bandages and held it in place while Jo pulled up her pants.

"It feels much better," she exclaimed.

We sat down, side by side opposite the blazing fire, our backs resting against the warmed rock and ate some more fruit, banana, mango and what Jo called 'monkey' fruit; weird-looking but quite tasty. However, what we really needed was some meat. I resolved to try and sort that problem later.

Whether it was the warmth of the fire or simply due to exhaustion from the last few days, we both nodded off.

I awoke as Jo tried unsuccessfully to get up without waking me, I have to pee she said, as she walked slowly and still obviously painfully to the designated area. (There was a natural alcove to the opposite side of the waterfall from where we entered that allowed the bodily fluids and such to be washed away).

I heard her gasp a little as her urine stung her raw wounds, similarly small sighs of relief when the area was washed with the cool water. She returned moments later and stood with her back to the cave entrance and looking at me said, "That feels so much better, it doesn't hurt quite so much."

"Well," I said, "seeing that you are up, why don't we explore our cave a little more, we don't have to go far, just enough to see what's back there, there might even be another way out."

"OK," she said, "I'll just put some more wood on the fire, its light may help guide us back."

Hefting my rucksack onto my back, I picked up my wind torch, cranked the handle a good few times and switched it on, the light was bright enough for what we needed and would stay that way as long as I cranked the handle every so often.

Jo picked up a small but stout stick, the only weapon to hand and I stuffed the pistol in my waistband; we ventured into the darkness of the cave.

Chapter 5

The cave floor was dry and dusty, quite devoid of animal tracks but there were signs of long ago habitation, we marked the dust with the stick, (an arrow shape pointing to the entrance) as we went just in case we found diverging tunnels.

As I swung the torchlight to and fro across the cave walls and floor, a flash of colour appeared; I stopped, Jo bumped into me and yelped.

"What's wrong?" she asked.

"Nothing," I replied, "I thought I saw something odd!"

I swung the torch light back over the walls to the right side of us and stopped its travel in amazement. There, in glorious colour and detail was a cave painting of a huge bull-like creature surrounded by human-like figures.

"Oh my god!" exclaimed Jo.

I could only utter, "Wow."

"This is really exciting. We are looking at something unseen for probably thousands of years," Jo continued.

We stood in awe for maybe five minutes, marvelling at the detail and bright colour of what was in front of us, a truly exciting and significant find.

We moved on, the torchlight bouncing off the cave walls in search of further wonders when all of a sudden it seemed to have lost its brightness, I cranked the handle furiously, it made no difference but when I looked at the beam of light, it nearly blinded me. I shone it back to where we had come from and it lit the area as before.

'How strange,' I thought, then I realised we had entered a huge cave and the torchlight just wasn't powerful enough to reach either to the roof or sides.

With Jo holding onto my waistband, we slowly and very carefully moved to the right side of what proved to be a huge cavern, I swung the torch only from the floor to the nearest wall, there were more paintings, all equally detailed and as colourful as the one in the passageway.

The cavern was circular in shape and eventually, we arrived back at our point of entry, we had during that journey seen a total of ten paintings and to our surprise and delight found a small pile of brush lights near the entrance to the cavern. (If we had turned left instead of right, we would have found them earlier)

We decided to try and light one of the brush lights and given that they were very old and very dry, we did not expect too much of it; we were totally surprised, not only did it catch fire easily with sparks from my 'firestone' but with the amount of light that it gave and also with the length of time that it burnt, the upper section appeared to be coated with a waxy substance. We lit another, sacrilege maybe but they lit our way and gave a much better light than the torch.

We walked freely now around the cavern, the ceiling was way above us and in the centre of the floor space was a flat-topped large rock surrounded, at a distance of about two metres on all sides, by ten smaller flat-topped rocks, one larger than the other nine, presumably seats.

This was truly an archaeologist's dream, for us it was a find of a lifetime.

The torches were beginning to burn closer to the upper binding that held them together, so we decided to return to our cave whilst we still had use of their light. The passageway back seemed so much bigger and less foreboding than on our journey in, we also discovered more paintings and what appeared to be a small tunnel on the right side but as our torches were burning down rapidly, we decided to leave exploring it for another time.

Jo was moving with more ease now and seemed happier in herself but I could still sense that she was carrying a weight on her shoulders that would take some considerable shifting. Whilst time and antibiotics could heal the physical wounds, only time and specialist treatment would heal the mental wounds as well.

We had been gone so long that our fire was down to embers and it took a little coaxing to come back to life, we dismantled one of the now almost burned-out brush-lights and used that as kindling which helped no end.

We once again sat side by side against the rock with the fire burning brightly in front of us and ate our meal of yet more fruit and once again I resolved to find some meat but as dusk was falling, it would have to wait until tomorrow.

I decided to try and find out more about Jo, I feared it would be a tricky subject, given what she had been through, so I started by telling her about myself and my reason for being in Africa.

She knew my Christian name and that I was working on the village water project but that was all, so there was more to tell if she wanted to listen, hopefully she would and then maybe she would tell me about herself.

She listened avidly and when I showed signs of tailing off, she urged me to tell more, I talked well into the night; being her senior by, I estimated about twenty-five years, I had a lot of tales to tell.

Gradually, she began to let slip details of her life, mainly in conjunction to something that I said about mine but it was a start.

I now knew her full name, Johanna de Klerk, pronounced Yohanna being South African; she was thirty-two, the daughter of a farmer in the 'Karoo' and she was a nurse specialising in paediatrics. She had been working with the medical charity for eighteen months, this was her third tour and at this moment in time, it would be her last.

Tiredness was beginning to take its toll and after stoking up the fire and the inevitable trip for nature's needs, we lay on the hard rock floor and fell asleep, again Jo had a restless night but the bouts of thrashing and moaning were short-lived.

Morning had broken and the daily ritual of stoking the fire and boiling some water to wash Jo's wounds had taken place. Once again, I was asked to apply some antibiotic cream to delicate areas which were healing nicely. The moss padding had definitely helped.

I was standing behind the water curtain looking out over the pool and wondering how I could find some meat when my view became a scene of horror.

Three youths, one several years older than the other two stepped out of the undergrowth. I turned to Jo, who was further back in the cave and motioned for her to be quiet.

The three were carrying rifles, they also had an assortment of other military equipment about their bodies and one had a small bow and a quiver of arrows, he also had what looked like a couple of chickens hanging on a strap.

I dare not move. I knew that with the darkness of the cave behind me, I could probably not be seen but movement may change that.

The three of them approached the pool, furtively looking around and obviously checking for signs of animals, convinced that all was well, they came right up to the pool's edge, the oldest and larger of them dipping a foot into the cool water, what followed I can only describe as excitement, they became very verbal and animated, the presumably older two haranguing the smaller one about going in the pool, I was transfixed.

All three stripped naked, it was obvious that they were intent on a dip in the cool water, the smaller was hanging back; the other two were goading him to go in. All three stood at the edge of the pool and the older two just dived in; when after a few seconds they didn't appear on the surface, the remaining youth moved forward as though trying to look into the water, too late, he slipped off the pool's edge and he too was swallowed by the deadly whirlpool.

I was aghast at what I had just seen but also grateful, for those youths to have returned to their camp and told others of their find would mean that we would have to leave the cave in short order.

Nature, they say can be cruel, also ruthless and yet beautiful, the pool just proved that.

Stepping back into the cave, I picked up my rucksack and emptied the contents onto the floor. I then removed my clothing, such as it was and walked to the cave entrance carrying my rucksack, Jo looked at me quizzically and asked what I was doing. I told her that I was going to collect the clothes and equipment left by the unfortunate youths, in case anyone else turned up and as I was going to get wet going in and out of the cave, I may as well be naked.

I tied one end of the rope around my waist and placed the other 'knotted' end into the cleft in the rock as my anchor point. I picked up my empty rucksack and put it on back to front.

I told Jo to stay out of sight, showed her where the pistol was (she said she knew how to use one) and asked that on my way back especially, she pick up the slack on the rope. I also added that if I got caught by anyone, she should throw the rope into the pool. That bit didn't go down well.

I cautiously edged through the water curtain and out onto the ledge, I couldn't see anyone nor did I see any reflections or shadows in the pool of anyone standing above the waterfall. I kept a careful watch as I worked my way to safety. Once on the forest floor, I gathered the items left by the youths as fast as I could, stuffing the clothes and smaller items including the quiver of arrows into my rucksack, it was bulging and heavy.

The three rifles and the bow I slung around my back, the rather well-used but still deadly machete I managed to attach to the rope by means of the leather thong that was binding the necks of a brace of 'Guinea Fowl', not chicken as I thought originally. They were stuffed into the rucksack.

I sanitised the area as best I could before struggling to fit the rucksack on my front as before, I needed it to fit that way in order to keep as close to the rock face as possible on my return journey. To fall into the pool even with the rope around my waist would probably mean certain death.

I managed it, god it was heavy and cumbersome but I didn't want to make two trips, the less time out of the cave the better.

I started to move slowly along the narrow slippery ledge, my back pressed as hard against rock as I dared but the rifles didn't allow me full advantage. Three quarters of the way round my left foot slipped, luckily most of my weight was still on my right leg and I stayed upright, my heart was in my mouth though and I took more than a few seconds to regain my composure. I could also sense Jo's fear, as the rope was pulled tighter.

As I emerged thoroughly soaked through the wall of water into the cave, Jo said, "Oh God, I thought you'd had it," she then broke into a fit of giggles.

"What's so funny?" I asked.

"You are," she said, "seeing your mostly white body bobbing about out there, stuffing god knows what into that rucksack of yours and then struggling to put it on and now, here you are standing in front of me drenched, armed to the teeth with a huge bulging rucksack on your belly and naked from the waist down. Oh, if only I had a camera."

"OK," I said, rather haughtily, "I won't do it again."

She looked at me and said, "I'm sorry I didn't mean to offend."

"I'm not offended," I said, "I would probably laugh too if I could see myself." Then I added, "A good dose of laughter can cure many ills, so I've been told."

"My grandmother used to say something similar, 'Lag is die beste medisyne'."[1] Said Jo.

"Afrikaans," I said.

Jo looked at me and said, "Jy verstaan Afrikaans?"[2]

I took a flyer on this and said, "Only the odd word or so, in my line of work you pick up lots of different words."

"I can see that I must be careful with what I say in my sleep," Jo replied.

Jo helped me off with my rucksack and carefully untied and removed the machete from the rope around my waist, the rifles and bow were then unslung from my back and I was able to get dressed.

---

[1] Laughter is the best medicine.

[2] You understand Afrikaans

Jo had by this time unpacked the rucksack and was busily investigating the contents of a paper-wrapped package, "Oh ho," she said, "mealy pap that will go well with the Guinea Fowl."

"Well, seeing that I did all the dangerous stuff, you had better get cracking." I said with a smile.

While Jo prepared the birds, I sorted through our booty. The clothes were not much but when cleaned they would be useful, the military contents were a few rounds of ammo on bandoliers, some wound dressings and ointment of dubious origin and quality, two reasonable knives and three water containers as well as the machete and three apparently AK47 rifles complete with full taped side to side magazines, all in all not a bad haul. The bow and arrows were the icing on the cake, provided I could hit something.

The meal that Jo prepared was sensational, the Guinea Fowl were cooked to perfection and when I told her so, she reminded me that South Africans were masters of the Braai. [3]

"Point taken."

The mealy pap in addition to the juicy meat really set the meal apart. Dessert of course, was fruit.

Now that my rucksack was empty and more importantly dry, I started to repack it; if we had to leave in a hurry, I wanted to take all I could carry and would not have time to pack.

Once more to my surprise and our delight, I found a small packet containing a sachet of coffee, a sachet of sugar and one of milk powder with a plastic stirrer, all courtesy of a 'Hilton' hotel somewhere. Needless to say, the packet was soon opened and the aroma of coffee was in the air as soon as the water was hot.

We stripped and cleaned the rifles as we sat by the fire, the flames casting a warm glow on our faces and with full bellies, we felt content. The rifles were old and battered but the mechanisms seemed to be in working order, Jo seemed quite at home with the rifle. She told me that living in South Africa, you had to know your way around guns and more importantly, how to use them. I didn't ask any questions.

We stacked our goods together in a ready to go pile so that in the event of the requirement of a swift exit, we wouldn't have to start hunting around. The rifles were loaded and chambered but with the safety on, the same for the pistol.

---

[3] Barbecue

Morning came without any night-time disturbances. Our breakfast consisted of the remaining Guinea Fowl and although cold, it was just as delicious. Jo's wounds were healing nicely and her bruises were beginning to fade.

We needed more wood for the fire and unfortunately, more food if we were going to stay much longer. We had enough of both for one day more but that would be it.

Chapter 6

A decision was made to once again venture into the tunnel but instead of going into the cavern, we would take the side tunnel that we had seen on the previous return journey.

We also decided that given the visitors of the previous day, we would take our belonging with us just in case anyone came along and found their way in to the cave. We stocked up the fire and made our way back along the tunnel with the aid of the remaining brush light, my wind-up torch was wound up and clipped to my waistband ready to go.

We decided that we would take two more brush lights from the cavern and use them during our exploration because not only did they give more light but that spiders and other such life, not that we had encountered any so far, would run away from the flames.

We made it to the cavern and picked up two of the brush lights and vowed that we would not take any more. We lit one of them from the now dying flames of the light that had shown us the way to the cavern, once again we were amazed at the amount of light it gave.

Backtracking, we entered the side tunnel and found ourselves moving up hill. We were hampered by our baggage as the tunnel was fairly small but we still moved fairly freely. There seemed to be a free flow of air and at times, the flame on the brush light would bend forward as though in a breeze.

We did however, encounter some cobwebs as we ventured ever deeper into the tunnel, the flames made short work of them and hopefully, the spiders that made them.

Jo was keeping up well and assured me that she was only suffering minor discomfort. We stopped for a few minutes and drank some water, we even tipped some over our heads.

"It seems to be getting steeper." She said and I agreed.

"Do you want to go back?" I asked.

"No, no," she replied, "we have come this far, we can go on for a while more."

The brush light was still burning brightly as we ventured further, about twenty five metres on the tunnel made an abrupt turn to the right and the climb became even steeper until we reached a dead end. We couldn't believe it, it didn't seem right! There were cobwebs all around the end of the tunnel and they looked as though they had been there for years, I touched them with my flaming torch in frustration. Poof! They went up in a sheet of flame revealing that the end of the tunnel was a few feet further on and appeared to be made of loose rocks and dried mud.

We were intrigued, making sure that there were no spiders waiting to take their revenge and having removed and set aside my rucksack, I moved up to the blockage. The mud was like concrete, so I asked Jo to pass me one of the knives that we had gained and the small trenching tool that I used for nature's deposits, from my rucksack. With those to hand and Jo holding the brush light, I began to chisel and chip away at the mud, it was slow progress but gradually I began to see results. After the first rock was removed, others were easier to remove but there was more than one layer.

The brush light was beginning to falter and having lit the remaining one, we had to make a decision, to carry on digging or return to the cave, we decided to carry on a while longer.

The ever-growing pile of rocks that we had jointly shifted were filling the passageway and Jo began painfully to carry them further down the incline to the bend.

I came to what appeared to be a wall of rock-hard mud that neither my knife nor trench tool would dig into and so laying on my back, I kicked it with both feet, a cloud of choking dust was my reward but something had happened, the mud wall had moved forward, I kicked again and again; each time it moved a little more, again and again and this time light came in around the edge of the mud plug.

It wasn't mud, it was a large rock with a mud-like patina, a soft sort of crumbly rock, I gave it a few more kicks; the softer rock crumbled away leaving a hard shiny surface of granite type rock. I then pushed it as hard as I could, it moved far enough for me to see bright sunlight and vegetation; seconds later, a current of air from inside the tunnel rushed out through the gap, stirring up a curtain of dust that had lain untouched for possibly thousands of years choking us both in the process, it made an eerie sighing noise as though it sensed freedom after many years in the depths of the mountain.

As the air cleared, I could see that we were on top of an escarpment looking towards steeply downward sloping ground. I could hardly contain my excitement. Calling back to Jo, I said, "Come and look at this." Wedging the rock in its partly open position with my trenching tool, I eased backwards into the tunnel and let Jo past, she was as excited as me.

"A way out," she said when she came back.

"Yes," I agreed, "but we need to make sure nobody finds the way in before we leave, it's too late to go today."

We managed to get the rock to sit back in the recess by digging the dirt out from the bottom edge, what it looked like from outside we didn't know but it was out of our hands anyway.

We retraced our steps down the passageway back to the cave, setting a few traps with some of the rocks that we had removed from the blockage on the way just in case of unwanted visitors. About a third of the way down, I noticed the brush light flame suddenly change direction, whereas up to that point it had bent in the direction of the newly discovered exit, it now flared straight up.

"Hang on a minute Jo, I want to check something."

I slowly moved back up the tunnel watching the flame as I did so, suddenly it changed its direction again. Carefully, I lifted the brush light to the roof of the tunnel. The flame flickered as though in a breeze. In the shadows, I could make out a small opening, just large enough for a man to crawl into and from where a faint current of air was flowing.

Satisfied with the reason for the flames action and the explanation of the escaping air at the exit, we continued down to the main passage making it just before the brush light burnt out, from then on it was wind-up torch only.

Back in our cave we washed, ate and made plans to leave early in the morning, we actually admitted to each other that we would be sad to leave this sanctuary.

I decided that we should only take what was totally necessary, it would still be a hard slog to civilisation and extra weight would take its toll.

The clothes that we had acquired from the unfortunate youths although washed or at least rinsed in the curtain of water that formed our door, still smelled pretty rancid, so we dispensed with all of them accept for a pair of cargo style trousers for Jo and a camouflaged flak jacket, which would do as a groundsheet if nothing else.

We inspected the three rifles closely and kept the two that were in the 'best' condition, the third one minus its magazines, I lowered into the whirlpool.

Rucksack packed, rifles at the ready, clothes and food prepared, we bedded down for the night.

(In a feminine touch, Jo folded the remaining clothes and placed them on a ledge close to the fire, "For future inhabitants," she said.)

Chapter 7

The curtain of water at the cave mouth was beginning to glow in the morning light. We were both awake and had been for some time, the excitement of leaving I suppose.

We ate a little fruit sitting behind that 'curtain of safety' and taking one last look at the pool and its surroundings, having washed our hands of sticky fruit juice and our faces of night-time sweat, we turned and picked up our belongings. I carried the rucksack with the machete wrapped in cloth strapped to its side and one of the rifles, Jo dressed in the rather ill-fitting pair of cargo trousers carried the other rifle and bow and arrows, we both also had full water bottles and a bandolier of ammo across our torso's.

I switched on my torch, cranked the handle a few times and we set off down the tunnel. We didn't look back.

Reaching the side tunnel, I cranked the torch handle again and took the lead in, the tunnel was quite narrow so we couldn't walk side by side. Jo followed my lead and my torch light while I called out as we reached the obstacles (traps) we had set the previous day.

Having reached the end of the tunnel, we removed our gear and mulled over our plan of action.

After moving the blockage far enough at least to get out, I would exit and check that all was OK, I would return and Jo would pass me the gear before coming out herself. With safety in mind, I suggested that I should give a password on my return just in case some undesirables were waiting to pounce and what she should do if I didn't give it, she laughed but agreed, "Boerwurst" [4] was decided upon.

---

[4] Farmers Sausage

The rock seemed more stubborn than the day before and it took some serious pushing and kicking but eventually, I managed to get my head into daylight, one thing for sure if anyone was in the vicinity, they would have heard us.

Little by little, the rock moved further and I managed to get my shoulders through, I could then see why it was so difficult. The rock was at an angle within a rocky outcrop and some smaller rocks had fallen into what was basically the hinge point, restricting the movement of the rock.

I scraped some skin off my chest and stomach as I wriggled through the gap enough to reach some of the small rocks and managed with the aid of a rifle butt and some serious sucking in of my stomach to allow the rock to drop back a little and take the pressure off enough to move them and release the exit rock. Free at last, I scouted around the area; no one in sight, I crept back to the tunnel exit and called out, "Boerwurst."

"Stop making me hungry and get me out," Jo replied.

Having gotten our gear and Jo from the tunnel, we took a moment to assess our surroundings and allow our eyes to adjust to the bright sunlight before resealing the tunnel exit and trying to make the area look untouched. Satisfied with our work, we took a drink and a bite to eat whilst studying the terrain for a way down.

We were on the opposite side of the ridge from where we had entered the undergrowth in order to avoid the encamped militia and so were heading in the right direction. Taking a sighting with my compass, I decided that a heading of 125 degrees (ESE) would seem about right and that hopefully given that it was more populated towards the east, we would find a road and some transport. We loaded up with our chosen gear and prepared for some serious walking, Jo assured me that she was fit enough and that the wounds had healed 'thanks to the antibiotics' so not to worry. I had my doubts.

The way down would be treacherous, the ground mainly loose rock and scree, so we would have to take our time. It looked as though we were about three hundred metres above the level ground although even that continued a gentle downward slope but at least the going would be easier.

It must have taken a good hour to reach the bottom of the ridge and we lost our footing a couple of times during that but we survived.

Another drink and short rest before setting off across gently downward grassy slope, taking advantage of any shade that was available along the compass heading, deviating slightly from the course as required, all the time keeping a watchful eye for predators of any sort. We were making good time, the ridge was way behind us but we never seemed to get any closer to what we could see in the distance in front of us. We were losing the light and would need to make camp out here in the grassland, thorn bushes would be advantageous as it offered natural defences.

We found a likely spot and with the machete formed an area that would give us some protection from wild beasts but unfortunately that didn't include mosquitoes (one problem we didn't have in the cave), we didn't bother with a fire, we ate the last of the fruit, drank some water and settled in for the night using the rather smelly flak jacket as a groundsheet.

Oh, how those mosquitoes feasted on us that night, we were slapping ourselves constantly, I don't believe I really slept at all, thank goodness we still had some 'malaria' pills left. However, getting one of those stuck in your throat with not much to wash it down with is no joke. Urgh!

We were getting ready to move when Jo said, "Don't move."

I froze, she carefully and slowly pulled the machete from its sleeve on my rucksack and then with speed that I hadn't seen from her before slashed at something behind me.

"OK, you can move now," she said, "it was a Mamba but it won't hurt you now." she said, lifting the snake's headless body with the machete blade. I almost collapsed with relief.

With that episode over, it was time to move on. The sun had begun its ascendency into a clear blue sky, sign of another scorching hot day, in which we needed to find food and by the end of the day, water but also hopefully safety.

We trudged on slowly, despite Jo's assurance earlier that she was OK for the trek, she was showing signs of pain; several times, particularly when on uneven ground she would gasp in pain but when asked if she needed help, she just glared at me and carried on. I really felt for her.

We had been walking for several hours, in and out of whatever shade we could find when we crested a small seemingly insignificant rise and to our amazement, there was a road. Oh joy! But which way to go? It ran, according to my compass North-South, not really the direction we wanted.

We decided on the southerly route, given that the capital of Mozambique was in that direction and although that wasn't our destination, it would probably be the best bet to find civilisation.

Our pace picked up as we walked along the tarmac, the fact that it was 'tarmac' as opposed to packed dirt indicated that it was a major route and so hopefully, we might be lucky enough to find transport. We had been walking for about half an hour when the sound of an over-worked diesel engine reached our ears, when we looked back the way we had come. We could see a huge plume of black fumes hovering above the road and a bus or lorry like vehicle in the thick of it, we looked at each other and grinned.

"Quick, drop the rifles," I said, "if they see them they won't stop."

I stood at the side of that road and in the best 'British' tradition stuck out my hand. You could hear the driver furiously crunching down the gears and slowing down the typically horrendously overloaded African bus but hey, what difference would two more passengers make.

The appearance of two white people and especially a blond white woman being one of them may have played a part in the bus stopping but after Jo got on and I followed carrying the rifles, the driver was obviously wondering if he had made the right choice, the passengers were probably thinking the same thing.

I gave the driver a handful of coins that had been lurking in my rucksack (I usually kept some to hand out to the kids) and struggled up the aisle to find something to hang on to. Jo had found a perch further up. The fact that the driver didn't start shouting at us meant that I'd either paid handsomely or he was just plain frightened.

The bus belched great black clouds of noxious fumes as it pulled away, mind you the smell of humanity inside the bus probably wasn't much better, not that we could talk but once some speed was built up, the breeze through the open windows although hot was wonderful. The bus rumbled along the road for probably twenty five to thirty kilometres before a sizeable town came into view, where after more gear-crunching and brake drums squealing in protest, we came to a stop at a very crowded terminus.

The passengers were anxious to get off and there was no way we could've stayed on even if we had wanted too.

One of the good things about the English language is that no matter where you are, someone will know some of it. An officious looking gentleman with a cap on his head was standing by what appeared to be the bus terminus office, the ideal candidate!

"Excuse me," I said to him, "is there a hospital near?"

Feeling important for perhaps the first time in a long while and in his best broken English he said, "Hospital, Good, OK." and then held up three fingers and pointed to the left.

I also held up three fingers and shrugged, he got the message and gesticulated walking, one, over road, two, over road, three, turn into road, then said, "Hospital" and gave the sign of the cross, which I presumed meant that it was run by a religious order and not that it was a place of last resort.

We followed his directions and apart from the good citizens of the town avoiding us like the plague, we arrived without a problem. However, mayhem broke out when we approached the entrance and from all around, there was shouting and a panicking security guard appeared pointing a rifle at us that looked a bit like the ones that we were carrying, although ours were shouldered.

From the midst of the melee, a man in a doctor's white coat appeared and calmed the scene, he spoke in clear authoritative tones to the assembled crowd and then turned to us.

He spoke initially in 'Portuguese' but when we said, "Sorry, we don't understand," he switched to English.

Chapter 8

"I am Dr Fernandes," he said, "how can I be of assistance?"

"We need some medical help, please. My colleague," I said pointing to Jo, "is in a lot of pain and we have been travelling for days to find help."

He looked at Jo in a professional but critical manner, noting her bruising and minor cuts and abrasions but not seeing any obvious major trauma, "You had better come in," he said, "but I don't allow weapons in the hospital."

"We can leave them in any safe place you like, we will make sure that they are empty, do you have a strong cupboard or cabinet?" I asked.

The doctor thought for a while and said. "Show me that they are truly empty and I will have them placed in a safe place."

We ejected the magazines, which I placed in my rucksack and racked the slides to eject the chambered rounds and offered the rifles to the doctor, the ejected rounds I placed in a trouser pocket.

The doctor turned and carried the rifles into the hospital, we followed. The hospital was clean and smelled strongly of disinfectant. The doctor obviously ran a tight ship.

We followed him into his office. His name tag matched the name on the door, Dr Ignatius Fernandes, Medical Director it said in bold letters. He bade us sit down and opening what appeared to be a large safe like door, told me to put the weapons including the bow and arrows inside; it was racked out with many mainly bare shelves. He then closed and locked the door. Seeing my quizzical look, he explained that the strong room is for holding the more expensive and critically needed drugs, adding that this is Africa after all. He then asked details of the medical problem.

Outside his office was a hum of activity, probably more so than normal because of the interest in the two foreigners.

43

Jo started to explain the scenario, that she was a nurse working for 'Universal Medical Access' (UniMed-A) a medical charity and had been working at a 'Makua' village.

Before she could continue, Dr Fernandes said, "Ah yes, it has been in the news, such a terrible tragedy, everyone killed and the adolescent children have disappeared, nothing left but burnt huts and half eaten bodies. No survivors. No witnesses, the carnage was only found two days ago."

"Not everyone was killed," said Jo. "We survived!"

Before she could say anything else, the Dr leapt to his feet, held a finger to his lips and walked to his office door, peering left to right outside of his office he then came back inside and shut the door firmly.

"You were there?" He asked.

"Yes," we said together.

"You must not tell anyone this," he said, "under any circumstances as long as you are here. If you are known as survivors, your lives will be in danger. There are many, shall we say informers who would sell you for a few 'Metical'[5] and the militiamen would probably attack us as well because we helped you."

"OK, we understand," I said, "but Jo needs urgent treatment."

I looked at Jo and could see that she was about to burst into tears, "It's OK," I said trying to reassure her, "you will get through this, I'll tell the Doc the story for you if you like, I know it's painful for you."

She looked me in the eyes and nodded, tears welling up, her fists clenching and unclenching, her body flinching in mental torment.

"Doctor," I said, "can you get a female nurse for Jo and have her taken to somewhere safe and quiet while we talk?"

He picked up the phone and hit a few buttons, after it was answered, a short conversation in Portuguese was made, and he put the receiver down. Less than a minute later, there was a knock on the office door and two female nurses entered dressed in full length grey 'nuns' habits with white veils covering their heads and spotlessly clean white nurses' aprons.

"Take this young lady to Ward six and stay with her until I arrive," he told them. "Let no one else in and do not talk to anyone else."

"Yes doctor." They said in unison.

---

[5] Currency of Mozambique

44

They stood either side of the now sobbing Jo and gently eased her from the chair. She looked at me as though for help.

"It's OK," I said, "go with these nurses, the Doctor and I will be along shortly. Don't worry you're safe. I won't let anyone harm you."

With that, she let them lead her from the room.

"Ward Six?" I asked the Doctor.

"It's a private room," he explained, "reserved for more important patients, she will be safe there."

I briefed the Doctor on the salient points relating to Jo's condition and the treatment that she had been having since then.

He was mortified, not at our medical treatment but at the brutality and inhumanity of her assailants. "One hears rumours," he said, "but an actual account by credible witnesses makes it undeniable. I think we had better take a look at your young lady 'sem demora'."[6]

"Before we see her, I have one important question to ask Doc," I said, "given the ordeal that she has undergone and the fact that she was raped multiple times, could she be pregnant? She has been bleeding quite freely but I don't know where from exactly."

"It's probably too soon to carry out any kind of test but I will see if I can ascertain the probability. There are of course drugs available now but we don't carry them here, being a Catholic Hospital." he added.

Ward Six was at the far end of the hospital, away from the noise and frantic activity of the public areas. In fact, it was more like a mini hospital in a hospital.

Jo was laying on what had to be the most comfortable, let alone clean bed in days but she was most likely totally unaware of the fact.

I went over to her and brushed my hand over her still wet cheek, she was staring at the ceiling but then she turned to me and a smile briefly appeared.

"It's OK," I said, "the Doctor's going to check you over, I'll be here and you have two nice nurses to help."

She smiled again and said meekly, "Staying."

"Yes," I answered.

The nurses helped her out of her clothing, giving a most peculiar expression at her choice of underwear. The Doctor said something to them in 'Portuguese' and they looked at me. I'm sure I blushed.

---

[6] Without delay

They fitted a hospital gown over her and then wheeled her on the bed to a small anti-room within ward six. It was an examination and minor operating theatre.

She was lifted with my help onto an operating table, I was told to put on a gown and scrub myself if I wanted to stay. I did as instructed.

The Doctor gave instructions to the nurses and they started loading a stainless steel trolley with an assortment of instruments and dressings, then they fitted two stirrup like attachments, one either side of the table onto which they each placed one of Jo's legs.

I stood beside Jo's head, comforting her as best I could.

The Doctor sat on a stool at the end of the table and started his examination of her pelvic area. One of the nurses who was closely assisting him was clearly quite shocked at what she saw, even with a surgical mask on, her eyes showed the signs.

The Doctor said to all in the room, "The trauma is quite extensive and will require some surgery to correct it, nerve damage may also have occurred."

He then said to Jo and me, "The antibiotic treatment that you have been using has started the healing process well but only specialist treatment will fully repair the damage. We do not have that capability here. You will need to go to a major hospital, probably to South Africa, given that's probably where your home is. I will however do what I can to make you comfortable for the journey and will write a letter for which ever hospital you go to."

He said something to one of the nurses who made a phone call and spoke in rapid 'Portuguese', then put the phone down and returned to the table.

The Doctor saw my concerned look and said, "Don't worry, I have just asked for some clothing for this young lady." He then carried on with his work.

"I am going to give you a large dose of 'Penicillin' he told Jo, I know that you have been taking tablets but this should make sure that no infection takes hold and I can give you something for the pain. It must be very painful to walk around with those injuries, you really need to rest but you also need to get that specialist treatment I mentioned earlier."

"Now my dear, could you give me a specimen of urine, I want to check for any bladder infection, the nurse will give you a bottle and show you where you can go."

The nurses helped Jo off the operating table and one of them led her to the toilet.

When Jo came out with her sample, the nurse took it and handed it to the Doctor who was obviously going to carry out the test himself. I could only guess why.

Before departing with the 'sample', the doctor told the nurses to attend to Jo's other injuries, by the time they had finished applying ointments and various dressings Jo looked like she had been in a major battle.

As Jo was getting ready to get onto the bed, there was a knock on the ward door, one of the nurses opened the door after checking through the peephole and took a bag from an unseen hand, it was an assortment of clothing for Jo, in fact it was a complete 'ensemble' although not exactly the height of fashion. As an added bonus, there were also a T-shirt, pants and trousers for me.

Whoever had ordered the clothes was a good judge of size, the clothes that Jo chose were almost a perfect fit.

Dr Fernandes returned and gave the results of the urine test, "No infections present," he declared, "your timely use of the 'Penicillin' paid dividends."

"Now, I have been able to arrange transport," he continued. "Mr Greenlove from your charity is sending a vehicle. A driver I am told will be here in about one and a half to two hours, so if you would like to rest until then please be my guests, ward six is yours."

"Mr Newman, if you would like to come with me to my office, I can return your equipment and I will give you a letter for whoever treats this young lady, just in case I am otherwise engaged when you are due to leave."

"I thought it best to answer your question privately," Dr Fernandes said as we entered his office, "the chance of pregnancy is there of course, I could find no trace in the urine sample but little time has passed since the event; it is not uncommon in these cases for nature to lend a helping hand but we can only hope for the best. I have made mention of it in this letter." he said as he handed it to me.

"Miss de Klerk is in a very fragile state and will probably need a prolonged period of treatment. I only wish that I could be of more help."

I shook his hand and thanked him for all that he had done and asked how much was owed and to where I should send the money. He said the bill is of no consequence and that he was only too glad to be of assistance. I made a mental note to send a donation as soon as I returned to my base.

The Doctor opened the strong room door, pointed to the rifles and said, "Even unloaded they make me nervous, please take them away." I duly obliged.

Carrying the rifles in my hands and the bow and quiver of arrows on my back to the shock and surprise to everyone I passed, I made my way to ward six to await our transport. One of the nurses let me in and then they both left saying that one of them would come back when the transport arrived.

About fifteen minutes later, there was a knock on the door and before I could get to it the door was opened from the outside and a waft of fresh coffee preceded one of the nurses carrying a tray covered by a cloth.

"Doctor Fernandes thought you might be in need of some refreshment." She said. I took the tray from her and thanked her and the doctor profusely. She then turned and left, closing the door firmly behind her.

I placed the tray on the bed beside Jo and lifted of the cloth cover. To my delight, I looked upon two cheese rolls, four 'Madeline' type cakes, and two cups with saucers, a small jug containing thick, sweet, condensed milk, two teaspoons and a pot of steaming aromatic coffee. I hadn't seen or smelled such wonders in days.

I poured the coffee into the cups and ladled in two spoonful's of the sticky condensed milk, stirring the spoon until it released the last drops of its sumptuous coating, salivating I might add at the thought of the deliciousness to come.

I offered Jo the first cup of coffee, she looked at me, still in a state of bewilderment. I coaxed her into taking a sip and then another, a smile came to her face as she savoured the taste.

"Good coffee," she said, "and look at those, I'm starving."

Taking the coffee cup from her hand, I replaced it with a cheese roll.

"Eat," I said and she did and ate the cakes, all four of them.

I ate the other cheese roll and sipped at my cup of coffee, trying to make it last. Jo finished her coffee and I then drained the contents of the pot into her empty cup, spooned in some more condensed milk, stirring it vigorously, handed it back to her. I'm ashamed to say that I scraped the last of the condensed milk from the jug with my finger, I needed the sugary hit.

Leaving Jo sitting on the bed dressed and ready to go, I headed to the bathroom to change into my 'new' clothes, preferring not to shock the nurses should one come in whilst doing so. To my delight, the bathroom not only contained a shower but soap, facecloth and towel, this was an opportunity not to be missed.

It was only when I looked in the mirror that I realised the state that I was in, still I could wait for a shave. Standing under that hot running water, the soap bubbles foaming as I lathered up was heavenly; when I turned off the water and had towelled myself dry and dressed, I felt ready for anything.

Returning to Jo, she seemed a little more aware, the food and coffee had awakened her senses somewhat and she was much more lucid and wanting to talk.

I explained what was going to happen in case she hadn't taken the information in before, she said that she understood and would be glad to go home. We spent the rest of the waiting time dozing, Jo on the bed and me sitting on a chair with my head resting on the side of her bed.

It seemed as though I had only just closed my eyes when I heard a knock on the door and it opened, a nurse came in followed by Dr Fernandes and another, younger white man.

Jo sat up and looked at the trio before saying, "Dr Tom."

The man smiled and said,

"Hello Johanna, I thought I had better come and get you!" Before approaching the bed and giving her a hug.

We had better get a move on, he said it'll be dark fairly soon and it's not the best road back to our base plus we have two new drivers and I am not sure how good they are.

The nurse and Dr Tom helped Jo off the bed whilst I heaved on my rucksack and gathered up the weapons. Dr Tom looked at me as though to say 'what the hell do you want with those?'

I simply said to him, "Don't worry, they're safe; it's a long story, I can tell you later."

Chapter 9

There was a Japanese four by four with two African men in the front seats waiting for us at the front of the hospital, they didn't get out to open the rear doors for us, unusual but not unheard of. I opened the rear passenger door and ushered Jo onto the rear seat, I then opened the rear door and placed in the weapons and my rucksack in the cargo area taking my time to ensure everything was tied down, making some apparent adjustments to my clothing afterward.

I was aware that I was being watched by the driver who was monitoring the rear view mirror, I closed the rear door and went to thank Dr Fernandes for his help and hospitality.

He was engaged in conversation with Dr Tom but broke off talking long enough to shake my hand and wish us a safe journey and Jo a speedy recovery. I left the two Doctors to talk and went and sat beside Jo in the car, I sat in the nearside behind the front seat passenger just in case we needed to make a swift exit, it's safer to get out on that side. No traffic.

I saw Dr Tom offer an envelope to the Medical Director who politely refused it. I then heard only snippets of a conversation in which the words 'inter-charity' and 'donation' were used, the Medical director then accepted the envelope, grasping it in his left hand he shook Dr Tom's with his right and watched as with Dr Tom on board, we were driven out of the hospital grounds.

It was obvious that Jo knew Dr Tom. He told me that he was the Assistant Medical Manager for Mozambique and was responsible primarily for the medical manpower.

Given his accent, I asked from where in America he was from, he said, "Actually I'm Canadian, it's a common mistake that people make."

I hurriedly apologised.

"None needed," he said and then turned his attention to Jo.

Jo answered his questions only very slowly and sometimes not at all, it was obvious that she was having difficulty processing what was asked, '*Dr Tom was trying,'* I think, '*to make a clinical evaluation, the questions were about random subjects but in a coordinated way.'*

We had been travelling for about thirty minutes further along the road that we had travelled in on and had passed a junction when the Dr shouted to the driver that he had missed the turning. The driver kept going.

Dr Tom shouted again and this time, the front seat passenger turned around holding a pistol in his right hand and said, "Not wrong," and shot the Doctor in the chest three times.

Jo screamed.

The shooter turned right around and pointed the gun at me, glaring at Jo said, "Shut up or he dies too!"

She stopped screaming and turned her attention to the mortally wounded Dr who was by now in the throes of death.

It was decision time for me. It was obvious that there had been some kind of information leak and that our days on this planet were running low. *'If they were taking us to where,'* I thought, then I didn't rate our chances very high.

I had never shot a man or even an animal before but it was a 'them or us' situation and I was determined that it wasn't going to be us.

The driver increased speed and the vehicle was bouncing over the potholes and ruts in the road.

I straightened myself up in my seat as though trying to get comfortable, I was aware that I was being watched by those in the front seats and as I moved, I carefully pulled my pistol from my waistband where I had put it whilst loading our gear into the vehicle.

I snicked the safety off as I pulled it out. Leaning slightly forward and holding onto the grab handle with my right hand, I pushed the muzzle of the pistol against the seat back behind the shooter in an area where I thought his heart (if he had one) should be and I squeezed the trigger twice. The noise inside the vehicle was deafening even with the windows open.

His body convulsed violently and then slumped forward, I lifted my arm and held the still hot muzzle to the back of the driver's head.

"Stop!" I commanded, he didn't. I hit his head with the pistol and shouted again. "Stop and pull up slowly or I will shoot you. You hear me!" He nodded.

I braced myself against the seat back, as the driver at first seemed to slow down gently, I saw his knuckles clench on the steering wheel and knew what was coming. He slammed on the brakes, hard. It was only because Jo was wearing her seatbelt that she didn't catapult over the seat and would probably have broken my arm in the process. I rewarded the driver with a hard clout with the pistol butt.

"Turn the engine off but leave the key in," I said to him, he did as ordered, "Now get out and move away from the car."

I opened the rear passenger door and climbed out while still holding the driver in sight, it was my undoing! My right foot landed on a loose rock and I twisted my ankle making me go down like a sack of potatoes, by the time that I had painfully stood up using the vehicle door as support, my left arm was hanging loosely by my side; the driver had seen his chance and was now kneeling backwards on his recently vacated seat, his right arm holding his dead colleague's pistol to Jo's head.

A smirk appeared across his black shiny face and he asked, "Where pistol?"

I didn't take my eyes from his gaze but said, "Down there" and pointed down with my right hand that was looped through the open door's window aperture.

The smirk became a broad smile that showed off a perfectly white set of teeth, his right arm began to move slightly back towards his body in order to avoid Jo's face, his intention was clear. I brought my left arm up sharply, my finger squeezing the trigger as the barrel reached the top of the driver's seat back, and the bullet took him between the eyes, his pistol never fired.

He was propelled backwards out of the car and when I had managed to hobble around to where he lay, a dark red pool was staining the dust at the back of his head. I leant down, picked up his pistol and placed it on the driver's seat. The (ex) driver was laying on the road, eyes wide open but the smile had gone. I felt no remorse. Jo was strangely silent, just sitting there looking straight ahead.

For some unknown reason, I decided to drag the driver's body to the edge of the road and place him near to where his dead colleague would soon join him. I grabbed him by his feet and proceeded to pull him around the front of the vehicle and off the road. It was not an easy task when you can only put weight on one leg.

That done, I opened the front passenger door and heaved out the shooter. That was easy. Using a T-shirt torn from the driver, I mopped the blood stains from the seat as best I could and then shut the door.

Hobbling to the rear, I collected one of the rifles, inserted one of the double taped magazines and chambered a round, making sure the safety was on and made my way to the front of the car, where I laid it against the driver's door.

Moving Jo into a front seat proved difficult, she was so traumatised that the only response that I could at first get from her was, "Dr Tom, he's dead." she repeated it again and again. I had to try a different tactic.

"Jo," I said, "We must get Dr Tom home, he needs to go home; if you get in the front with me, he can lay on the back seat." Eventually, she looked at me and nodded.

"All go home." She said.

I eased Jo on to the front seat via the driver's door opening, I didn't want her to see the dead bodies lying in the dust, strapped her in and then lay the body of the dead doctor across the rear seats and strapping it in place as best I could with the seat belts before placing the rifle between Jo and myself in the front, butt down on the floor.

I started the 4X4 up and with pain coursing from my injured ankle as I pressed on the accelerator did a 180 and drove to the turning we should have taken over an hour ago, we would be hard pushed to make it to Marrupa before nightfall.

I drove as hard and as fast as I could, I found that by keeping my ankle stiff and moving my leg to adjust the accelerator, the pain was bearable but braking was another matter and I had to resort to left foot braking whenever possible, even going as far as knocking the 4x4 out of gear to be able to apply the brakes until we reached the outskirts of Marrupa, where I slowed down looking for signs pointing us to Universal Medical HQ.

Jo was still awake and seemed to be becoming more aware, so I asked her if she remembered the way; she could not but then a stroke of good luck, about fifty metres ahead, a truck with the UM logo coming from the opposite direction turned right, down a side road, we followed it and eventually, it led us into the UMA compound.

Our arrival caused consternation when out of the vehicle came only two people and both white!

I shouted for help and people came running, it was when I opened the rear door and they saw Dr Tom lying dead that the questions really started.

A large bald-headed man had emerged from the building that we had parked in front of and although it was now quite dark, the lights from inside the building were bright enough to illuminate our vehicle and the body lying on the back seat.

"Who the hell are you?" he asked, "Where's Dr Naismith?"

"I presume you mean Dr Tom," I said as I pointed to the body on the back seat.

"What! Oh my god. Get him to the sick bay." he instructed to everyone and no one in particular.

"It's too late for that." I said.

Looking at me then through the vehicle, he asked, "Is that Nurse de Klerk?"

"Yes," I replied, "and she really does need help. She needs very gentle handling, she's totally traumatised as well as injured."

A team of several people were now taking the body of Dr Tom on a stretcher into the building, I turned to Jo and was encouraging her to come away from the vehicle when two of her nurse colleagues appeared and took over, they gasped at the blood over her clothes and were at first relieved and then equally appalled when I told them that it wasn't Jo's blood but that of Dr Tom.

"So I presume you are the chap responsible for the return of Nurse de Klerk." the bald headed man said to me.

"I think we helped each other to get this far if the truth be known," I said. "I'm Martin Newman. You are?"

"Oh yes sorry, James Greenlove, area manager for 'Northern Mozambique'," he replied, "I think you had better come inside, it would seem that there are a lot of questions to ask and to be answered."

"Sure, but what about Jo?" I asked.

"She's in good hands, we have a full medical unit here, staffed around the clock. It's not only field work that we do. You can see her in a while."

I retrieved my rucksack, the rifles and the bow and quiver of arrows from the now cooling 4x4, the engine ticking as the hot metal de-stressed.

"What in the name of hell are you doing with those?" Greenlove exclaimed.

"It's a long story and I will explain over a cup of coffee if you would be so kind." I said to him, a grin on my face.

He led the way to his office, while I hobbled along behind. His office was a functional affair but nicely furnished, I guess a man of his status had to hold court with various government officials and powerful entities in order to operate effectively.

"Take a seat," he said and then picking up the phone, ordered coffee.

I placed my rucksack and weapons alongside a comfortable looking chair and plonked myself down in it.

"Hmph!" exclaimed Greenlove, as though it was not the chair that I should have taken but tough, I wasn't moving.

"You have a security problem," I said before Greenlove could open his mouth, "those drivers that you sent to collect us, killed your Dr and threatened both Jo and me, although I get the impression that Jo was wanted alive."

"No chance!" Greenlove said forcefully, "all of our staff are thoroughly checked and that is especially so in the case of local labour, our security is top notch."

"OK, so tell me how that given we have only been on the radar for just over a day, the very people who are sent to pick us up try to kidnap us! Dr Tom told us that your drivers were new, that he said that was one of the reasons that he came along to pick us up."

"Whoever employed those drivers signed the doctor's death warrant."

Greenlove flushed with either embarrassment or anger, I wasn't sure which but it elicited a torrent of denial.

"I did not order Dr Naismith's death, for god sake, he was a friend and a damn good doctor and as I have already told you, our security is top notch."

"Well, somebody must have let slip that Jo and I were alive and needed transport, it was arranged by this office, wasn't it?" I asked.

"Yes," he replied. "I organised it myself."

"It couldn't have been from the hospital in Metarica because although Dr Fernandes had told you where we were, he didn't have any idea how you arranged your transport and as yet, the company that employs me have no idea that I am alive, let alone needed picking up."

There was a knock on the office door and a young black man came in with a jug of coffee and a plate of biscuits.

"Put it down there, Joshua," said Greenlove pointing to the small table adjacent to where I was seated. As 'Joshua' turned to leave, a man in a doctors coat appeared in the doorway, 'Joshua' hurriedly exited.

"Ah, Dr Wilson," said Greenlove, "how is Nurse de Klerk?"

"Johanna is in a bad way," the doctor said, the tone of his voice indicating his irritation at the innate formality used by Greenlove towards his staff. "I have given her a sedative to allow her body and more importantly, her brain to rest. She will need several weeks at least to recover and then maybe never fully."

"Her physical injuries are quite severe and will possibly require reconstructive surgery, not something that we can do here."

It was then that I remembered the letter that Dr Fernandes had given me to pass on to the hospital, I removed it from my rucksack and passed it to Dr Wilson, who opened it carefully and having read it said,

"Thanks this is most useful and by the way, I'm Richard and I would like to thank you for all the help that you have given to Johanna, we are actually a tightly knit team despite the way that some come across," looking at Greenlove as he spoke.

His sarcasm went over 'Greenlove's' head.

"That's OK," I said, "no thanks needed, we helped each other; by the way, I'm Martin. When will I be able to see her?"

"We haven't finished our examination yet and given the contents of this letter, we have a little more to do. I will let you know. I would like to talk to you before you go, for background info, if that's OK."

"Sure, she will need all the help she can get, she was gang-raped, brutally by the sounds that came out of that hut, both vaginally and anally for sure and possibly orally, so besides possible pregnancy, there are always the other diseases to take into account. Jo never told me the actual events, I guess she was just too traumatised but I know what I saw and heard and the state that she was in when I carried her out of that hut."

Richard nodded knowingly and left the room, Greenlove just sat there open-mouthed.

"How could this happen?" he eventually asked, "We have taken extensive precautions to make sure that our staff are safe and yet you are telling me that it's far from it!"

"It's possible that your medics being in that village when it was hit was just bad luck but the transport scenario was not and I will tell you why."

I related to him the whole episode of our journey from the hospital in Metarica, to the point of our taking over the car and driving back to his office.

Greenlove was horrified and apologetic. About halfway through my account, I saw a flicker of thought on his face, it seemed that he realised that his security had been compromised and was not as 'Top Notch' as he thought. My suspicion was confirmed when he said,

"We have been having a problem with local labour recently, some of our drivers have left and we have had to engage new staff; we get them from an agency in town all pre-vetted, so our security checks are perhaps not as deep as they should be, that will be rectified forthwith."

"I think that maybe the agency you use should be investigated as well, it would be quite easy for them to be controlled by shall we say 'undesirable elements', I think also that it might be prudent to inform Doctor Fernandes of the incident, he was most insistent that we did not reveal our involvement in the massacre while at the hospital, for fear of retribution." I told him.

"Yes, point taken, I will inform both the authorities and the good doctor first thing in the morning, it's too late to try and get hold of anyone now."

"Can I use your phone?" I asked, "I need to inform my company that I am still around."

"Oh yes, please do, I should have offered earlier, it's all quite a shock and I am not functioning as well as I should be." He then pushed the phone towards me and said, "You need to press nine for an outside line."

I took a swig of coffee from the cup that I had filled earlier, it was bitter but welcome and dialled the number of my boss in Cuamba, it was answered on the fourth ring.

"Mc'Quary," the voice said.

"Hi Mac, it's Martin," there was silence for a few seconds then that 'Aussie' twang, positively shouted down the phone said,

"Who the fuck is this, some kind of arsehole joke? You wanker!"

"No, no, it's me Martin! And I'm coming to claim that beer you promised me, you 'Aussie' git, can't you tell who I am from my dulcet 'British' tones?"

"Fuck me. Where are you? The authorities said there was nothing left, that the village and everything and everyone was destroyed. They wouldn't let us near due to security reasons. Huh, what fucking security?"

"I'm at a medical facility in Marrupa, I brought out another survivor, she works for the medical centre."

"A nurse then, hmm, is she pretty?"

"Yes, she is pretty and pretty badly injured as well; those bastards gang-raped her, she's pretty fucked up and to add insult to injury, I reckon it was the same bastards who had another go at us on the way here today."

"I'll be there first thing, where are you staying?"

"I'll find a hotel, in town." I said, looking at Greenlove as I said it, he nodded and said,

"I will arrange a room for you."

"But don't make it too early, I want to see how Jo is and I guess the authorities may want to speak to me about a few things."

57

"No problems mate, see you about midday. By the way, glad to hear you're alive you 'Pommie' bastard. Just let me know where you will be."

"If you come to the Uni-Med facility, it's on," I looked at Greenlove, who shouted at the phone.

"Avenida Silvia Da Costa, it's about three kilometres from the airport."

"OK, got that," said Mac, "see you tomorrow." I put down the phone.

"If there's nothing else, I'd like to see how Jo is," I said to Greenlove. "Can I leave those weapons in your care? I don't think or at least, I hope I won't need them anymore."

"Yes, yes I will get them locked up in the gun safe."

"Great, in that case you had better have these as well." I said and I removed the other magazines, the bandoliers, machete and the driver's pistol from my rucksack and placed them on the table next to my empty coffee cup.

Greenlove never uttered a word.

"Right, now can I see Jo?"

He locked his office door after we entered the corridor and then led me through a series of double doors into what was obviously a seriously well-equipped medical centre. Staff were chatting at the nurse's station when we entered but hurriedly resumed their tasks on seeing Greenlove.

"Where is Nurse de Klerk?" he asked one of the staff at the counter.

"Bed 7," the nurse replied, "Richard," she corrected herself, "Dr Wilson is with her."

I followed Greenlove through another set of double doors into the ward and then to the room at the end of the ward, Room 7 it said above the door.

Richard was studying a strip of paper, presumably a printout from one of the machines that Jo was hooked up to. He looked up as we entered.

"Hi," I said, "how is she doing?"

"She's resting, as I told you earlier. I gave her a shot to help her sleep and we will continue to monitor her stats, we have taken blood and urine for testing and redressed her wounds. Dr Fernandes was correct in his diagnosis; she will need extensive rehabilitation and possibly reconstructive surgery to her genitalia. Those bastards really caused some damage."

Greenlove had heard enough.

"I need to get back to my office," he said, "to put away those items that you brought with you and to arrange a hotel room, come back when you are ready to leave." he said to me and turned and exited the room.

"Pompous prat," Richard said, "he might be a good administrator but a fully functioning human being he is not."

"What's the prognosis on her recovery, doc?" I asked.

"Too early to say, I'm afraid but how about a cup of coffee and you tell me the full story, it may contain some info that can be of help for her treatment."

"How long have you got?"

"As long as it takes, she's one of our own."

I went to Jo lying there helpless on the bed, wires and tubes attached all over her, she looked so frail, I touched her hand and gently squeezed it but she didn't respond, I bent forward and whispered in her ear.

"Jo, it's Martin, don't you dare give up, we have gone through so much to get here and you have got years ahead of you. See you soon." I kissed her cheek and then left the room with Richard.

"There will be a nurse in attendance all night," he said, "if anything changes they will call me, plus I have my rounds to do anyway."

The duty doctor had an office and we were now sitting in it, drinking hot sweet coffee, Richard produced a couple of packets of those glucose biscuits that are so popular in Africa, they didn't last long.

I narrated the story to the best of my ability from the initial onslaught on the village, through the trek to the forest and the close encounter with the militia, the discovery of the cave and the wonders inside, the way out through the tunnel onto the ridge, Jo's quick action that saved me from the snake, the bus ride, Dr Fernandes and finally the ride to where we were now.

"Wow some story," was all he could say.

"I think Jo will need more help than we can give her but who knows maybe a couple of days rest will speed things along, she will still need surgery though."

"I know that I mentioned it before but if she is pregnant, would that not cause her more harm, mentally, I mean?"

"Yes probably, it's a grey area, not one that I can really advise on but there are drugs that can be administered to take care of that, if you know what I mean!"

"Do you have them here?"

"Normally we do but I've just used the last ones on a very important patient."

"Oh. Thanks." Changing tack I said, "I'm really sorry about Tom Naismith, he seemed a nice guy but it was all so sudden, there was nothing I could do."

"He was one of the good ones, a damn good doctor and a very pleasant and caring boss, not like that idiot you have just been with. I'm glad you got the bastard that shot him, he deserved it."

"Right, I think it's time to get you to that hotel and me back to work."

We left the office and as I hobbled along, Richard said, "I think I'd better take a look at your ankle before you go, we can't send you out in that state."

I was motioned to an examination table where after removing my right boot and carefully examining my slightly swollen and purple-coloured joint, he said, "It's just badly sprained, I can dress it but if I do you probably won't be able to get your boot on, so my advice is to leave it as it is. I will give you some painkillers, rest it whenever possible, your high ankle style boot most probably saved you from a lot more damage."

He then helped me to ease my foot back into the boot.

We proceeded to the nurse's station and there sitting in front of the counter was my rucksack with a note clipped to it with the address of the hotel. Greenlove had gone home.

"See what I mean," Richard said. "Not a fully functioning human being. I will arrange for a driver to take you there now."

"I hope this driver is a lot more reliable than the last two." I joked.

"So do I," he replied, "he has to take me home after my shift as well."

I arrived at my hotel safely and with minimum fuss was issued a key and pointed towards my room.

The room was clean, the air-conditioning on and set at a very acceptable 23 degrees. I was just too tired to shower, I removed my clothing and lay on the bed. I don't even remember my head touching the pillow.

Chapter 10

A ringing telephone woke me, "Hello," I answered.

"Newman. It's James Greenlove. A gentleman from the authorities will be at my office by 0900 hrs and he wishes to talk to you. I have arranged for transport to be at your hotel at 0845, please be ready."

"What time is it?" I asked, my room was in darkness due to the blackout curtains and I felt as though I had only just fallen asleep.

"0745," came the reply. "Be ready." And then the line went dead.

I sat up and swung my legs over the side and stood up. The pain hit me like a sledgehammer and I fell back onto the bed,

"Shit!"

In my haste had forgotten about my ankle, I tried again, this time favouring my injured ankle and hobbling carefully to the bathroom.

The hotel had thoughtfully provided toiletries but the razor would be of little use on my several days of growth but at least I would smell good even if I didn't look it.

Showered and dressed and with my rucksack over my shoulder, I managed to make the lobby, grab a couple of breakfast rolls and a coffee to go just as the transport turned up.

We pulled into the compound to see Greenlove and a well-built but athletic-looking dark-skinned man in a military uniform walking from the 4×4 that I had driven back yesterday.

The driver pulled up in front of the office building and as I exited the car, Greenlove approached and made the introductions,

"Newman," he said, "this is 'Coronel De Almeida' of the Counter Insurgency Force, he wishes to speak with you regarding your exploits."

"Sure, no problem." I acknowledged the Coronel with a nod.

"I suggest we go to my office," said Greenlove as he perspired under the rising heat.

We were just climbing the steps to the building when a small truck drove into the compound, sounding its horn loudly. I turned as did the others to see it pull up sharply and the driver's door swing open, a deeply tanned ginger-headed man got out.

"It's 'Mac', my boss," I explained, "now the fun starts."

Mac strode over, ignoring Greenlove and the Coronel and grasped me in a bear hug, "Jesus, you old bastard, I thought you were a goner too!"

"Mac, I would like you to meet Mr James Greenlove. He's the General Manager here and Coronel De Almeida of the Security Forces."

"Coronel?"

"I think it's the equivalent of our Colonel." I said. "The Coronel wishes to speak with me about my exploits."

"Great, I arrived in time then, save you having to repeat it to me later," he then turned to the others, introduced himself and shook their hands. Greenlove cringing in agony as Mac's vice-like grip squeezed his finely manicured hand.

As we entered Greenlove's office, I asked how Jo was.

"As well as can be expected, I'm told," was the answer I received.

"I would like to see her after this meeting, if that's OK."

"We can ask the medical staff if it's appropriate," he replied.

Coronel Almeida was obviously used to taking charge of events and when we had all sat down, he asked me to 'tell my story', he had heard it from Mr Greenlove but he wanted to hear it from me.

"Second-hand information is often unreliable." he said.

I began. As before I only narrated the salient points, I didn't want everything that we had seen to be heard at this point.

I described the arrival of the militia into the village, the sound of gunfire, the screams and shouts of alarm of the villagers and presumably, the medical staff and my colleagues.

When I described the large black man who was involved in the assault on Jo and who I thought was probably the leader of this gang of murderers, the Coronel became highly interested. He asked me why I thought this was so. I told him that more than anything, it was the way he acted, that the others in his murderous cabal seemed to be in awe of him.

"Maybe it was his booming voice," I said.

"Ah, 'O escolhido' without doubt." the Coronel said.

"Sorry, I don't understand."

"O escolhido," he repeated, "The Chosen One, leader of the Espada de Cristo militia. They are responsible for many deaths, we have been chasing them for a long time."

"Sorry to ask but I don't speak Portuguese, what does 'Espada de Cristo' mean?"

"The Sword of Christ."

"Why the Portuguese names? Although I don't speak it, I can recognise it being spoken and I don't recollect Portuguese being used when they raided the village."

"It was most likely that they spoke 'Makhuwa', it's a Bantu dialect, most commonly spoken in the north. You must remember that Mozambique was a Portuguese colony for over four hundred and seventy years and mainly Catholic and therefore, God-fearing nation. By use of the language of the colonial masters and the religious connotations associated with them and the church, lesser educated people can be easily drawn into these evil groups," he explained.

"I know where they are or maybe where they were camped," I continued, the Coronel's eyes lit up,

"Tell me more!" he commanded.

I told him of nearly falling into their hands by rushing to the smell of the cooking food and of the sudden realisation of danger when hearing his voice and the rattling of rifles.

"You are not to leave this place until I say," he commanded, "tomorrow I will bring maps and you will show me where this encampment is."

"We will wipe this evil from our land." And then in a completely different tone of voice he said, "Please continue your story."

I told them of the escape into the undergrowth, of the finding of the sanctuary by the pool and of the waterfall but I didn't describe the wonders of or even the access to the cave.

The gaining of the rifles and ammunition was also another area that I was most careful about, I described the arrival of the three militia men and of their swimming in the pool, I don't think he believed me when I told him of the 'whirlpool', however he let me continue.

It was when I described the events in the 4×4 coming back to UMA HQ that he suddenly seemed to take real interest again.

"Ah yes," he said. "You have just told me that the doctor was killed by the man sitting in the front passenger seat, yes?"

"That is correct," I replied.

"So if he had that pistol," pointing to the one on Greenlove's desk, "and your rifles were unloaded and in the back of the truck, how did you manage to shoot him through the back of the seat?"

I leant over to my rucksack and pulled from it the pistol that I had found in the ruins of the village.

"With this," I said, placing it on the table.

I thought Greenlove was going to have a heart attack, Mac looked a bit green as well but the Coronel was unmoved, although I sensed that if needed he would have moved very quickly, a smile lit upon his face.

I slowly picked it up and ejected the clip and the round in the chamber and slid them over to the Coronel.

"Interesting. A 'Makarov PB'." he said, "And how did you come by this?" He asked, holding the empty pistol in his hand.

"I found it in the ruins of the village the day after the raid. I think it belongs to the Chosen One as you call him, I noticed a holster on his hip as he came out of the hut."

"I vowed to return it to him or at least the contents of it if I ever saw him again."

"Ha, ha, you might not be that lucky, very few people have lived to tell a story such as yours and it would seem that they are already on your trail, you might have more luck with one of those AK's."

He thumbed the bullets from the clip, "Only three?" he said enquiringly.

"Three would have been enough, of course there were six to start with but that fracas in the 4x4 used half of them."

"One for him in the right place would do the job but if that failed, then one for Jo and one for me. There was no way that I would have let her fall into the hands of those bastards again."

Greenlove, his face flushed, blurted out, "But that would be murder."

"Actually I believe 'Murder/Suicide' is the correct term and I agree but if you had witnessed what I had, then I suspect you would do the same thing."

Mac, who had been unusually quiet up to now, simply said, "Too right."

"It has been noted that 'O escolhido' does or did have such a weapon, of course his finger prints will no longer be visible, very unfortunate." The Coronel interjected.

"Well, I was hoping to keep it in case our paths ever crossed but I guess that is not going to be the case now." I said.

The Coronel slipped the empty clip into the pistol body and slid it back across the table to me.

"I think we can allow you a small souvenir. Of course, it would be unlawful to possess such a weapon in your country."

"That I believe answers all of my questions. I shall return tomorrow with maps and you can show me where this nest of vipers is hidden."

He stood up. "Gentlemen," he said, "until tomorrow." Turning to Greenlove he said, "I trust you will provide someone to place those weapons in my car." Then he walked out.

I took the chance to check on Jo and hobbled off along the corridor and through the double doors to what I had previously assumed to be the Nurses' station, in fact it was obviously the out-patient reception desk.

The whole room was a seething mass of humanity, people were jostling for attention and the nursing staff were in the thick of it.

I edged my way to the reception desk and asked for the duty doctor, I explained to the nurse that I had come in with Johanna, as that seemed to be what they called her and would like to see how she was progressing.

"If you can just wait a few moments," she said, "I will see if that's possible."

"It had bloody well better be," I replied.

She disappeared into the ward area and came back a few moments later with a dark-skinned man in a white coat hot on her heels.

"I'm Max," he said, "Richard left a note saying that you would be coming in, he also wrote a lot more about you but we don't need to go into that."

"Nothing too bad, I hope!"

"No, quite the contrary," he replied, "shall we go through?"

As we approached Bed 7, he explained that the nurses were just making Jo comfortable.

I noticed that a bundle of blood-stained bedding was placed to one side. I looked at Max in horror!

"Don't be alarmed," he said, "it's perfectly normal at this time."

Ah, I suddenly understood.

"Monthly flow?"

"Yes." He answered.

"Well, at least she isn't pregnant." I did however wonder if it was just that time or Dr Richard's intervention.

One of the nurses came out with the blood-stained bedding in a plastic bag.

"You had best incinerate that," Max said to her.

"Yes Doctor," she replied and hurried off with her package.

"You can't be too careful with items like that."

My suspicion was true but I was thankful.

Jo was still lying comatose on a now clean white sheet, dressed in a light grey and white checked hospital gown, her feet and lower limbs were covered in a thin blanket. A thick band of wires and tubes ran from the complex looking stack of monitors and electronic machinery and were attached to her.

An oxygen tube was attached to her nasal passages and she was breathing deeply. Other tubes ran from under the blanket into bladder like bags hanging onto the bed framework.

Max, seeing my concerned look said, "It's all perfectly normal, standard in these situations. We are monitoring her vital stats and so far, all is normal. Of course, should anything change, we will be on it straight away." Adding, "We look after our own, regardless of the effort or strain that we are under."

I could only murmur, "Thanks," adding, "I have only known her a few days but we have been through so much together, I can't bear the thought of her not pulling through, she has her whole life in front of her and to think that her condition was inflicted basically by members of the very community that she was trying to help, is beyond belief."

"Those who did that to her are not rational human beings, they are people who are often embroiled in tribal as well as religious fervour and when whipped into a frenzy by these Warlords, they cannot see that what they are doing is wrong. They are, if you like 'high on bloodlust'. I don't wish to justify what they do; I'm just trying to explain why. They will in the end have to answer for their crimes one way or another."

It was obvious there was nothing that I could do for Jo and to hang around would only hamper the medical staff's work, so grasping Jo's hand I once again whispered words of encouragement into her ear, brushed my hand lightly through her hair before leaving the room.

"Don't worry," Max said, "if there are any changes, we'll be on it and we will let you know."

Mac was waiting in the corridor with my rucksack on the floor beside him,

"Thanks." I said picking it up.

"I've put your pistol in there," he said, "now, let's go for a beer or two, you look like you could do with one and anyway if you don't, I sure as hell do."

Driving out of the compound in Mac's 'Ute' as he called it, he said,

"Greenlove booked us a couple of hotel rooms for tonight, made a great deal about it though and was quite implicit that he wasn't paying the bill, especially as he had paid yours last night. I told him that 'Life Source Exploration' paid its own bills and to invoice me for your stay last night. He's a real weirdo."

"You should hear what his staff think of him." I said and left it at that.

We were in the same hotel that I had stayed in the previous night, I even had the same room.

After checking in, I went down to the nearest pharmacy and with an advance of cash from Mac, I purchased a decent razor, other toiletries and then decided that while I had the chance, I should replenish the items used from my rucksack. The pharmacist was most obliging and only queried my request for the 'Penicillin' tablets, he also recommended a particular brand of antibiotic cream.

Leaving the pharmacy, I found a 'Cavalheiros Outfitter'* which sold every item of clothing that I required, the clothes from Dr Fernandes hospital had served their purpose but there is nothing like your own.

Back at the hotel and after a long shower and sporting a razor-nicked face and new clothes, I met Mac in the bar for a few beers.

The first two went down without touching the sides and it was only when on his third that Mac broached the subject that had been eating away at him and he approached it in his typical Aussie way.[7]

"You 'Pommie bastard', you nearly gave me a fucking heart attack, calling me like that, those bloody wankers at the ministry told us that everyone was dead, same as the other village, chopped up and burnt mostly they said and that if your body was not there, then you'd probably been taken either by the scavengers or being white maybe as a hostage but they didn't think you were still alive. But then you call me in the middle of the fucking night, alive and well. Jesus."

I took his comments on board in a light-hearted way, I'd known Mac a long time and it was just his way of expressing himself, no malice in it.

"What do you mean?" I said, "Same as the other village?"

---

[7] Gentlemens outfitter

"Oh shit, yes of course, you probably don't know, that murdering bunch of bastards hit the village that Dicky's team were at, killed everyone, chopped off Dicky's and Pete's heads. The bastards. I'll do the same to them if I ever get the chance."

I was dumbstruck, as a small outfit, we lived in each other's pockets, more like a band of brothers than workmates. They would be sorely missed.

We spent a long time in the bar, not even bothering to go to the restaurant next door, just burger and fries and then more beer.

I don't remember what time I went to bed; I only know that it was dark.

Once again, morning came round too soon, the alarm call which I had thoughtfully arranged before going to the bar, sounding loudly in my head somewhere.

I sat up and lifted the receiver.

"Good morning, Mr Newman," said a cheerful voice, "this is your 7 o'clock call."

I ruffled my hands through my hair and gingerly put my feet to the floor, not bad, the pain was going but, ugh, my mouth was as rough as sandpaper, where's that toothpaste?

Breakfasted and waiting for the call from Greenlove who had told Mac that he would call when he was advised of Coronel Almeida's time of arrival, I sat in the foyer reading the English language copy of the 'Carta de Mozambique' newspaper when Mac bounded through the hotel entrance doors.

"You managed to get up then!" he said.

"Yup, breakfasted and ready to go," I replied, "I suppose you've been out there creating havoc."

"Nah, I decided that seeing I was at a loose end, I might just as well try and drum up some more business, early bird catches the worm so to speak. Coffee?" It was a rhetorical question.

The call from Greenlove came through at 0945, apparently the Coronel had been waiting for the maps to arrive and he was not happy with the delay, so best not to keep him waiting at UMA.

We hailed a taxi and were there within fifteen minutes, just as the Coronel arrived with his team and a bundle of maps.

As the Coronel's men were laying the maps on the small conference table in Greenlove's office, I asked him how Jo was that morning, he answered in what I can only describe as detached terms.

"Nurse de Klerk is in the care of the medical team and I am sure that they are caring for her as required."

A small-scale map of the area in which the village was situated was spread across the table and weighted down on the corners by use of items from Greenlove's desk, much to his disapproval I sensed.

The village was pointed out to me and I was asked to indicate the route that Jo and I had taken.

It was a North-oriented map and so easy to plot but the scale was too small to distinguish any salient points, another map was produced and laid on top, larger scale but of a much smaller area.

Once again, the village was highlighted for me by one of the Coronel's staff although I had already located it myself. With the aid of a rule from Greenlove's now largely empty desktop, I plotted a line roughly South East until I spotted what looked like the rocky outcrop that Jo and I had spent the night on.

I then further ran a line in a similar direction to the edge of the map, another map was produced and laid on the top of the existing one. I explained that although I was using a compass bearing on the map, we had in fact moved from areas of shade to shade and not stuck to that bearing.

Starting from the area closest to that of the previous map, I once again followed a rough South East heading until,

"Yes."

I arrived at an area that not only indicated rising ground but also vegetation, we had by that time according to the map scale travelled close to thirty kilometres not a great distance by normal trekking standards but given Jo's injuries, it was remarkable.

The telephone on 'Greenlove's' desk rang, he picked it up and said in officious tones,

"Greenlove," he listened for a few seconds and then said, "you are to proceed as instructed, let me know when the aircraft departs." He then listened again to the voice on the other end of the phone before saying, "No that will not be happening. 'Naismith' yes, the documents have been processed, there should not be any problems on that score." He replaced the receiver.

Now came the tricky part, trying to estimate how far we had walked before smelling those cooking fires.

I estimated that we had probably been following the edge of the forest about an hour before we smelled smoke and heard the sounds, given the scale of the map and working out our walking pace plus a little extra to where the camp might be. I placed a finger on the map.

Coronel Almeida looked at the area indicated and said something to one of his staff in a language that I didn't understand, the man produced a file of what appeared to be aerial photographs from a briefcase and skimmed through them until he found what he wanted and then passed it to the Coronel.

"This area," the coronel said, "is where you say the camp is and this photograph was taken only three weeks ago, you can see by the date here," he said. "No camp. See."

"Well Coronel, I can only tell you what we heard and smelled, that is definitely the right area."

I had been looking closely at the map and I could clearly make out the ridge on the other side of the rising ground where we had exited the cave.

"Maybe they have only recently moved in. Do you have any more 'photos' of the area?" I asked.

The Coronel instructed his staff member to hand over more 'photos', who laid them on the table in sequence.

Looking from left to right, I could see no trace of a possible camp but I did see at the far right what appeared to be a burnt out village.

"What's this?" I asked the Coronel.

"That village was destroyed, probably by these bandits about two months ago," he replied.

I picked up the photograph and studied it carefully and said to him,

"Coronel, this area," and pointed to the amount of flattened ground leading into the village, "I presume this is where they came in."

"Yes and where we also came in and went out, it leads to the road to Metarica, the same road that you might have turned on to."

I was about to place the photograph back onto the table when a feature on it caught my attention.

"Coronel, I assume your people searched the area around the village thoroughly, for survivors and such."

"Of course, very thoroughly!" He replied, almost to the point of indignation.

"On foot or in vehicles?"

"On foot, we could not have gathered vital information from inside a vehicle."

"Well," I said showing him the photograph, "those look like vehicle tracks to me and they appear to go from the village into the forest."

He grabbed the photograph, stared at it closely for a long while and then uttering a torrent of what I can only assume were expletives followed by orders to his staff, prepared to leave.

"Thank you gentlemen, you have been most helpful but I have to organise some troops."

His staff dutifully followed him from the room.

"Well," exclaimed Greenlove, "he has a bee in his bonnet but at least I have my office back."

"I'll go and see Jo then," I said to Mac, "and then I reckon a spot of lunch would be in order."

"Great idea," he replied.

Before I got out of the office, Greenlove said, "It will not be possible, to see Nurse de Klerk, that is. She is on her way to hospital for further treatment."

"Why, what has happened?"

"Nothing has 'happened' but we are not equipped for her type of injuries and so the decision has been made to send her to a facility that has."

"Why didn't you tell me earlier?"

"It was none of your business."

"What do you mean none of my business? Where has she gone?"

"That also is none of your business, you are not her kin nor did she express a wish that you be informed as to her whereabouts but I will tell you that she is currently being flown to South Africa."

"You bastard! You know damn well what we have been through together and you are also aware that she was in no fit state to express a wish to inform me or not of her departure either."

"They're right, you know. You're not a fully functioning human being."

Greenlove looked at me and said. "I do not care what you or indeed anyone else thinks of me, I have a job to do and regulations to abide by and I carry out those tasks to the letter and in full compliance."

"Mr Newman," he continued, "I wish to thank you for your time and efforts in assisting Nurse de Klerk to return to us, I appreciate that it may have been at considerable personal cost to yourself but that business is now over. Now if you would be so kind as to leave my office, I have much to do."

I left the office, Mac trailing in my wake.

We were just passing the doors to the treatment area when I stopped, looked at Mac and said,

"Can you give me a few minutes? I just want to thank the staff for their help."

"Sure, I'll be in the Ute, take your time."

I pushed through the double doors and my rage seemed to evaporate, the clinical smells seemed to having a calming influence.

I saw Max standing at the foot of one of the beds in the ward and raised my right hand to him. He saw my signal and indicated five minutes.

Having finished with the patient that he was attending to, he signalled with his arm to follow him into the duty doctor's office.

"Shut the door mate," he said as I entered the office. "This is about 'Johanna's' transfer I presume! I guess Greenlove was his usual diplomatic self, the pompous ass."

"Yup and I'm bloody fuming. I realise that legally I have no right to any info but common courtesy would not have gone amiss."

"I can understand your feelings completely, we knew that she would have to be moved to a more appropriate facility at some time but even we were unaware that it was happening so soon. We received instructions early this morning that a Medevac flight was on its way and that Johanna was to be shipped out but not only that, 'Tom Naismith's' remains were to go on the same flight."

"I would have liked to goodbye to her, even if she didn't respond she might have heard me. Have you any idea where she is going?"

"Afraid not, it's all hush hush, need to know basis and we apparently do not need to know."

"Is there any way you can think of that would help me track her down?"

Max thought a while then said, "If you write a letter and address to Johanna care of UMA and give it to me, I will put it in the company mail system, maybe that way it will get to her. Make sure you put your contact details in."

"Great idea, I'll do it now, do you have any stationary?"

Max produced some writing paper and an envelope from his desk drawer,

"I'll leave you to it," he said, "the company Head office address is written on the desk calendar. Address it to Johanna there. If I am not back before you finish, leave it in the drawer and I'll sort it for you."

"Thanks, Max. Thank you and all the team for all that you have done. Sorry to have met you under such circumstances. If we ever meet again, the beer is on me."

We shook hands and Max left the office.

I sat in the doctor's chair and began,

Dearest Jo,

You cannot imagine my surprise and disbelief on being told that you had been shipped out without my being allowed to say goodbye.

After all that we had endured together, it was a stab to the heart, clearly some people have no feelings at all.

I am not allowed to be told where you are as that information is for next of kin only.

I can only hope that wherever you are, you are receiving or have received the finest treatment possible and that you are either on the road to recovery or once again fit and well.

Although our time together was only brief and full of adversity, I believe we formed a bond that will last a long time.

Should you wish to meet once again, I can best be contacted via email. My address is maartin1065@hotmail.com.

Your fellow cave dweller,
Martin.

I folded the letter and placed it in the envelope and sealed it and marked it 'Private', addressed it to Miss J de Klerk. C/o Universal Medical Access at the address that was written on the calendar.

Max was nowhere to be seen, so I placed it in his desk drawer and left the office.

I exited the UMA building for the last time with Mac at the wheel of his Ute.

We stopped off at the hotel to grab a quick bite and clear our rooms before heading off back to Cuamba.

"That bloody hotel stung me for another night's stay, said as it was after eleven it was a new day. Robbing bastard, bloody receptionist probably put it in his pocket." Bemoaned Mac.

It took three and a half hours to reach Cuamba and the familiar confines of the Life Source compound. Apart from the occasional expletives shouted loudly by Mac at various other road users, it was a quiet and uneventful journey. The truth being that I didn't feel much like talking.

I think Mac understood but it didn't stop him from suggesting that we should have a few beers at his to celebrate my homecoming. I politely refused on the grounds that I was knackered, maybe tomorrow.

Chapter 11

Mac operated Life Source with two teams each consisting of two teams, a drilling team of which I was part of and the installation team who would follow on after the borehole was drilled and water found to fit the outlets and troughs.

I was the only member of my teams left after the murderous spree of O escolhido and his militia. Mac told his sponsors that there was no way that he was going to send his men into the bush until the government had either put paid to those murderous bastards or would give us an armed guard.

However, he told us that he wasn't paying us to sit on our arses until they did, so if we wanted to be paid we had better spend our time checking and if necessary polishing the 'bloody' equipment and if those buggers hadn't sorted the damned militia out by then, we'd be checking and polishing again.

The other teams' members, Pete T, Jonno, Mick and Dave gave me a soft ride on this, whether it was because of my recent 'adventure' or because as Mac kept reminding them that I was an old Pommie bastard I don't know but I put them straight. If you can do it, then so can I. I told them.

Evening conversation around the compound cookhouse cum bar revolved around my adventures and the apparently 'Pretty Nurse' who had saved my life. Typical Mac to put a spin on everything,

"The stories you tell, you should have been a politician." I told him.

We had been cleaning and polishing so to speak for five days, when late in the morning of the fifth day, Mac burst out of his office carrying an ice cold six pack.

"Blimey, this looks good." Mick said.

"Bloody momentous more like," Jonno chipped in, "beer this early in the day."

"They've got the bastards," he shouted as he strode across the hard-packed dirt, "right where you said they were. Wiped out the bloody lot. Got that Escol what's his name as well."

"How do you know that?" I asked.

"Just had that bloody General Almeida on the phone, here have a beer, enough work for the day, I reckon it's a reason to celebrate."

It was on the headline story of the main evening news.

Standing behind a lectern and surrounded by other military types and facing a press corp, the Prime Minister declared that the 'Espada de Cristo militia' and it's barbaric leader known as 'O escolhido' had been found at their camp and destroyed by our valiant 'Security Forces'.

"The action had been carried out under the command of 'Coronel Jorge de Almeida' and followed several weeks of investigation and information gathering. This action gives notice to all that this government will not stand idly by and allow our citizens and foreign visitors to be terrorised by these gangs of barbarians."

"I now hand you over to 'Coronel de Almeida' who will answer your questions."

The coronel fielded a barrage of questions from the assembled press but never once indicated that any information relating to the location of the camp had come from an outside source.

"Bloody good job too if you ask me," said Mac, "at least you won't be on a hit list."

The Coronel did however mention that several villagers had been rescued although some had been killed by their captors during the fighting and would receive assistance to return to their normal lives.

Six days had now passed since I had written the letter to Jo and although I didn't think that she might be recovered enough to send a reply, I hoped that somebody might do so on her behalf. I checked my inbox for an email, no such luck.

"OK, give it time," I said to myself.

Mac had decided that with the militia out of the way it was time to start the program again and that subject to any more hostilities over the next few days, Pete T and Jonno with their associated local labourers would head back out to the villages, Mick and Dave would follow two days later.

I was required to remain at base to help interview replacements for those of us who were no longer available and to assist Mac with the tricky problem of dealing with the relatives of those unfortunates.

"Not my idea of a fun job." I told Mac.

"Nor mine, mate," he said, "but you were in the thick of it and may be able to answer some of their questions better than me."

What could I say to that!

I did however convince Mac that each team should have a sat phone and should either call or at least text every evening after completing the day's work in order to monitor their safety. If that had been in place prior to recent events, Jo and I would have been found much earlier and Jo at least would not have suffered so greatly.

The next two weeks were, for me at least, 'hell'. Having to deal not only with questions from grieving and often tearful relatives but to then pack and organise shipping of my deceased colleagues belongings to those bereaved.

I made a decision and told Mac.

Mac was in his office, deep in conversation on the telephone when I went in. He indicated me to take a seat and shortly after that with the words to whomever he was talking too of,

"Right, I'll send you the ticket info and see you in three weeks. Cheers." he put the receiver down.

"What's up mate?"

"Mac, I've been mulling things over for a while and I've decided to sling in the towel, I'm getting too old for this malarkey, I'm gonna go home and put my feet up, maybe even take a long holiday."

"Whoa, you can't do that, I've got three new blokes coming in three weeks to join your team and I need you to train them not only in the way we operate, but in how to deal with the locals."

"Sorry, I've made my mind up, that fracas that I've just been through has made me realise that my time is running out and I want to enjoy a bit of life before I turn up my toes."

"Blimey, that's a bit morbid, think about it, what are you going to do in that cold wet country of yours? You'll soon get fed up with warm beer and bad weather, let alone you'll feel lost without your muckers to keep you on an even keel."

"I'll be fine, I've got my flat that I haven't lived in properly for years, that needs decorating, my car is still in the garage, if it hasn't rotted away. There's a pub just down the road and the quayside in front of my window, how could I possibly get bored?"

"You will, mark my words. Aside from that, you're going leaves me in the lurch, I'm gonna have to get another bloke on top of the three I've just organised."

"OK, if it's any help I'll stay around until the end of December but I want to be out of here by then. I'll train them in our methods and make sure that they understand how to communicate with the villagers but then that's it."

"Ha, you might have changed your mind by then, going back to 'Blighty' in the middle of winter. Christ mate, I reckon you've lost the plot."

"Nope, I've made my mind up, so you had better organise my ticket."

The following weeks passed quite quickly, the new recruits were all experienced in drilling and soon adapted to our methods, it was communicating with the villagers and especially with the 'village chieftains' that caused the greatest problems.

It took some considerable effort, particularly with 'Steve', to make them understand that although we were carrying out the work on behalf of the local government, the village Chief had to be made to feel that he was in control and that we were working for him.

"It can also take a lot of patience and powers of persuasion to drill for water in the right place and not just next to the 'Chief's' hut because that is where he wants it." I told them.

I checked my email inbox every day in the hope that Jo or even someone on her behalf had sent me something to at least indicate that she was alive and well. Nothing!

I convinced myself that either the letter hadn't got to her or that she was still traumatised and undergoing treatment somewhere.

'Christmas' arrived and Mac in his usual inimitable way had organised us all a slap-up meal but it was after the meal that caused me the greatest shock.

We had finished dessert and the beer was flowing freely when Mac stood up and called for silence.

We all looked at him in anticipation but instead of his usual toast to the company, the staff and its achievements he strode over to me and laid his hands squarely on my shoulders.

"This old bastard," he said, "is leaving us as you all know and nothing I say to him will change his mind, so being 'Christmas' and all that, I've decided, being the generous bloke that I am, to give him a present. I have in my hand here," he withdrew an envelope from his shirt pocket, "A ticket home, 'Business class',

I might add," and looking at me said, "your flight leaves the day after tomorrow, I know it's not the end of the month but don't worry, I won't dock your pay."

Everyone clapped and laughed, I just sat there, dumbstruck.

Mac had arranged transport to take me to the regional airport at 'Nampula',

"Can't afford the time to take you on a day out, short staffed," he said, a grin on his face, "got work to do."

I had packed all my belongings into my rucksack, I didn't have much, didn't need to, just a few personal items and some clothes for a couple of days.

My emergency medical items that had been so invaluable during my 'adventure' as it was known, I would leave for the team members to squabble over, my well used 'Leatherman' multi-tool and folding trench tool I gave to 'Jonno', who had had his eye on them for some time. They had a certain personal bond with me but airport security is rather picky about what you can take on as hand-baggage, so best left in good hands.

Mac stood by the taxi that had arrived to take me to the airport, shook my hand and said,

"I still think you're crazy, if you get really bored you can always come back you know, I need someone to make the tea!"

I laughed and said, "Thanks but no thanks. I have a parting gift for you though," and passed him a small brown package, "open it when I've gone. You never know it might save your life someday." and I got into the taxi and told the driver to go.

I looked back as we exited the compound gates. Mac had already opened the package and was staring at the 'Makarov'.

Part 2

Chapter 12

I had been home for a little over two months, my flat had been completely redecorated, my car serviced and polished to within an inch of its life and I was now staring out of my living room window across a wind and rain swept road at the boats in the marina rolling on a swell.

Lymington is a quaint Georgian town in Hampshire and on a summers day is packed with tourists, a real buzz can be felt but today in the cold wet weather of late February, it's downright miserable.

'Maybe Mac was right,' I thought to myself.

Still no word from Jo, I was beginning to think that perhaps she had decided that the past experiences that we had shared were best left in the past.

Thinking of Jo however brought back memories of the cave and it's beautifully drawn and coloured paintings.

They should be brought to the attention of academics, who could study them before someone else happened upon them as Jo and I did, I mused. Not everyone would treat them with the same reverence as we did.

'That's it.' I thought. Now, how do I go about it?

A search of the net soon gave me several leads but which would be best? Archaeology societies exist in many countries but very few seemed to have a worldwide remit. I should I suppose contact the Mozambique authorities but I'm in the UK! Hmm, maybe if I contact one of the universities that have an archaeology department, they might put me on the right track.

A search on 'Google' soon came up with 'Winchester', which is just up the road from Lymington. I made a call and was put through to the Head of the Department, Dr Nick Trulade.

He sounded interested in what I told him and a meeting was arranged for the following week.

My gloom was suddenly lifted, I once again had a purpose in life.

My appointment with Dr Trulade was scheduled for 2:15pm, which was great for me, the journey from my flat to Winchester would, I reckoned take about forty-five minutes, it was approximately fifty kilometres but then I hadn't been to the university before so I allowed extra time to find it and park the car.

Winchester is a city, not a town, by means of having a cathedral, which apparently has the longest nave in the U.K. and was many years ago the capital of 'England', it is now the county seat of 'Hampshire'.

The city is a mixture of both the incredibly old and very new architecture in abundance and the university campus reflects this also.

I parked my car in the closest car park that I could find to the university office and made my way onto the campus.

On arriving at the reception desk, I was delighted to find that Dr Trulade had organised a visitor's pass for me and a short wait later, he arrived to meet me.

We wandered through a myriad of passages, Dr Nick Trulade explaining the various departments of the faculty and other college buildings as we went.

We entered his office, which as I had imagined was wall to wall in books and papers but unlike on the TV examples it was neat and tidy, everything appeared to be organised.

"Take a seat," he said.

I sat in an overstuffed armchair facing at an angle to his desk.

"I don't do formal," he said, "I'm Nick and you are?"

"Oh, just call me Martin," I replied, I liked him already.

"Right, what's this about and how do you think I can be of help?"

I gave him an abridged version of our journey, from the escape from the Makua Village to the finding of the cave and its wonders.

He sat listening and not interrupting until I had finished.

"Well, that's some story! Do you have any proof of your find, photos perhaps?"

"No, I am afraid not, as I explained we left the village with just my rucksack and what was in it and that did not include a camera or phone. I would like to say that my travelling companion would confirm the events but not only was she badly injured, she had been repeatedly raped and was in a confused state to say the least. She has now been taken to a hospital somewhere in South Africa but I do not know where it is."

"Hmm, not actually a good start really. I believe you but in order for my department to progress any further, I need some kind proof."

"I cannot provide proof. I can, however, give you names of persons who helped us in Mozambique and of a Coronel, that's Colonel in our army, that I assisted in finding the militia that we had escaped from and were subsequently put down by the 'Security Forces' in that area. Although he did not see the cave, nor did I tell him of its secrets I did tell him of its existence and of the waterfall. I realise that this is not much but it's all I have."

"Well, that's a step in the right direction. Obviously, we could only carry out any research on your story with the blessings of the Mozambique authorities but that would be obtained by the university governors and admin department and so we would have to convince them first that it would be a viable project and not a wild goose chase.

The 'whirlpool' is also intriguing, it's outside my knowledge, I've heard of them obviously but I have no idea about how they work. However, I have a colleague who is a 'Professor of Geology' at 'Southampton University' who might be able to assist. Actually, she specialises in 'Tectonics' but I guess she can advise of somebody to help if she can't."

"That would be great. Do you have her number?"

"Better than that, I'll give her a call, she may be lecturing but we'll soon find out."

He dialled the number and after four rings, it was picked up.

"Professor McLaren."

"Hi Lisa, its Nick Trulade, how are you?"

"Oh, hi Nick. Not bad, just up to my neck as usual!"

"Sorry to bother you but I have a chap in my office recently back from Africa with a tale of cave paintings and a whirlpool."

"Wow! Is he to be believed?"

"He has no proof but he has given me some leads. The cave and paintings are right up my street, there are similar in that region but the whirlpool is not something that I know about, that's why I called you."

"My speciality is Tectonics as you know but I can certainly find someone to help, I would be interested to talk to this guy."

"He's here in front of me, I'll put you on the speaker-phone and we can have a three-way."

"Hi, I'm Lisa, you are?"

"Martin, Martin Newman."

"Pleased to meet you, well actually to be more correct, pleased to talk to you."

"Likewise," I said.

"OK Martin, tell me about your find. Nick, please join in when you want to."

I related the story to Lisa the same as I told Nick and received the same reaction.

"What a pity you haven't any photos! But tell me about this waterfall and whirlpool."

"OK, the waterfall emerges from the cliff face, right out of the rock from a mouth like gap, it's about three metres wide and about a metre down from the top of the cliff, there is no river visible up above. The water drops into a pool that is about eight metres in diameter but only a little water flows from the pool.

The pool is encircled by sheer walls of rock for about three hundred degrees. I was curious as to why so little water flowed from the pool, so I threw a stick in expecting it to disappear into an underground channel at an edge but what happened was that it was quickly drawn to the centre and disappeared like going down a plughole."

"If there is this whirlpool, then how did you find the cave?" She asked.

"A medical necessity and another freak of nature. Jo, my travelling companion needed some padding for her wounds and I had read somewhere about a tribe that used a moss as an absorbent pad. There was moss growing beside the waterfall and I was going to use that. Just swim across and get some, I thought. That was before I discovered the whirlpool.

As I was pondering how to collect this moss, we heard a strange gurgling sound and noticed the pool level drop a few centimetres before rising to its original level again, well that was strange enough but I also noticed that when the level dropped, it exposed a ledge around the left side of the pool. Wide enough to walk on and get to the moss.

I did just that. I actually had to reach in behind the waterfall to get a large clump of moss and that's when I discovered the cave."

"Wow!" They exclaimed together.

"Fascinating," added Lisa. "Whirlpools or Gyres as they are commonly known are quite prevalent in the oceans and are usually caused by the ocean currents. What you have described is very unusual and sounds quite intriguing.

The fact that there is no over-ground river above the pool indicates that the river is actually subterranean and that the waterfall and the pool have probably been caused by a movement of the rock strata which is why there is a sheer face surrounding the pool. Did you notice any rock debris in the vicinity?"

"I didn't go looking for anything other than food or firewood but I can't say I noticed any large rocks, the whole area was covered in thick vegetation apart from the area immediately surrounding the pool," I replied.

"One item that is puzzling me," said Nick, "if, as you say, the militia swept into the village killing everyone and leaving your companion for dead, how come you survived unscathed and are here to tell the tale?"

"A call of nature."

"Pardon!" Nick said.

"Exactly that, I was just about to exit a clump of Thorn bush after relieving myself, when I heard the approaching vehicles and the sound of gunfire. I carefully retreated to safety and kept out of sight. To have emerged would have been suicidal."

There was silence.

"Well," said Lisa, "as much as I believe you, without any tangible proof, I think I would have a very hard job to persuade the governors to fund any field work and I suspect the same would go for Nick's as well."

Nick agreed.

My mind was racing, trying to think of a way to overcome this impasse when an idea suddenly popped into my head.

"I presume that universities have 'School holiday's'?" I asked.

"Well yes, although we don't call them that," answered Nick, "Why?"

"Well, I could go back to Mozambique and take some photos but, I wouldn't like to go alone, for safety reasons, I might slip and fall into that pool for instance but if one or even both of you came along then you could get whatever evidence you needed.

Taking on board what you have said about your universities not funding any field work, I have a proposition to put to you and them.

If you are prepared to come with me, perhaps in your holiday time, I will fund your airfare and accommodation costs on the proviso that your respective employers refund me those costs when you have the proof of my story."

"That's worth looking at," Nick said, "I could go to the governors and put it to them but whether they would go for it I honestly don't know. I can't say that I have heard of anything along those lines before, although, large companies do help fund our field trips for sure."

"Likewise," chipped in Lisa.

"You will need a visa for Mozambique and they are quite expensive, depends on the type that is required but I would try for a tourist visa.

I would also advise that you keep the reason for the trip private, if the authorities get wind of the possibility that the trip is for archaeological or geological reasons then I suspect that they would want huge sums of money to allow you in and probably take the whole thing out of your hands anyway.

I've not had dealings with the Mozambican government personally but I have with other African politicians and I know how they operate, no reason why the Mozambicans would be any different.

My old employer is still out there and I'm pretty sure that I could get him to organise any equipment that you will need along with local transport and such.

He would probably send a letter of invitation if one was needed for visa purposes."

Lisa said, "Look guys, I've got to go, class in ten minutes. Nice to talk to you Martin, I'll see what I can do this end and get back to you via Nick. Bye, Bye Nick." And she was gone.

"OK, seems like a way forward," said Nick. "I'll talk to my governors and see what they say, an answer may not come very quickly though."

"That's no problem, I'm retired, time is something I have plenty of at the moment but the longer you leave it, the greater the chance that someone else may happen upon it as we did."

"Point taken."

Nick led me once again through the myriad of passages to the main reception area where after handing back my visitors' badge, I was free to go.

The journey back to my flat somehow seemed longer, I don't remember anything that happened other than feeling totally and utterly deflated.

I had gone to 'Winchester' full of hope, false hope possibly and now I was paying the price.

Chapter 13

A full week had passed and I was at a loose end, pondering as to whether I should attempt the trip to the cave alone and even if I should forget the idea completely when the telephone rang.

"Martin," I announced into the mouthpiece.

"Hi Martin, its Nick Trulade! Sorry I've taken so long to come back to you but trying to get anything organised around here takes ages.

The governors have given tentative approval for an investigative trip subject to certain conditions being in place."

"OK, that's great. I was beginning to think that it wouldn't happen."

"Right. Apparently being an employee of the university and going on a foreign or indeed otherwise engagement that will be of benefit to the university, means I have to be funded directly by them in order for the insurances to cover.

They are also very apprehensive about not requesting formal permission from the government of Mozambique, I explained to them your reasons for keeping it quiet at the moment.

They are however, willing to grant me leave of absence (during the Easter break) to engage on a fact-finding holiday, provided I do not mention or involve the university in any way.

As for the costs, they have indicated that reimbursement of any funds that I might expend should my holiday bear fruit would be looked upon in a kindly manner, their words not mine.

I have spoken to Lisa and she is going along the same track on this but still waiting for an answer. Hopefully with Winchester agreeing, Southampton will also follow, as your find could benefit both Uni's."

"That really is good news. My offer to stump up the airfare still stands if you need it.

I know 'Easter' is late this year but time is short and without a visa, we can't go anywhere so that's a priority. You can apply online but then have to send your passport to the Mozambique High Commission.

Hopefully it won't take too long.

I will call Mac, my ex-boss and ask him to set things up his end, I don't think he will say no.

He's an Aussie, full of bluff and expletives but a great bloke at the end of it.

You'd best give me a list of gear that you need and I'll pass it on to Mac. That way we won't need to take anything out with us that might arouse suspicions at customs and immigration."

"Right, I'd better get started. I'll let you know when I hear from Lisa and what dates we can agree on. I presume you are still flexible?"

"Sure, I can go anytime. One thing to bear in mind, it's the end of the rainy season out there, it will be hot and humid, so you will need light clothing, a raincoat and strong waterproof boots."

"Looking forward to it already."

"As soon as you give me the dates, I will get my visa and the airfares organised."

"I'll be in touch. Bye."

My mood had changed dramatically, time for a call to Mac.

Mozambique is two hours ahead of GMT, that makes it 5:20 pm, Mac should be in the office with a bit of luck, I dialled the number and several long seconds later I heard 'Aussie' tones.

"Life Source, McQuary speaking."

"Hi Mac, its Martin."

"Well bugger me, I knew you'd get bored but I didn't think it would be this soon!"

"Oh, I'm not bored, well not any-more and before you ask, I don't want my job back."

"That's good because I've just employed a new tea-boy."

"Ha ha, very funny! You remember what I told you about my little adventure! Well, I'm coming back with some academic types to discover more and I wondered if you might use your considerable expertise and charming Aussie ways to help us."

"Jesus mate, what they been feeding you over there? Bullshit I reckon."

"I'm hoping to be out over Easter time but there's a list of stuff we'll need as well as a place to stay or at least an address to register as staying at.

Because it'll be at the end of the rainy season, I reckon the waterfall will be too dangerous to negotiate, so we'll have to get in the way Jo and I came out, which means climbing a wall of scree."

"So, you're going to need ropes then?"

"Yes and other climbing gear, probably Ice axes or something similar, to lock into the loose crap and help us pull ourselves up."

"Ice Axes! Where the fuck do you think I can get those? This is Africa, not bloody Switzerland."

"Oh, you'll think of somewhere, I have every faith in you."

"There's that bullshit again."

"We'll need powerful lamps, the type with battery belts would be best and some general camping gear as well but I'll send the list later when it's fully drawn up."

"Hey! I haven't agreed to help you yet."

"I know but you wouldn't let a mate down, would you?

Did you get those Sat-phones because we might need one of those as well, just to call you to pick us up?"

"Bloody hell, I think you had better go before I say something I might later regret."

"Thanks Mac, I'll send the list and arrival dates later. Bye."

Two days later, I had a message from Nick on my answerphone, Lisa would be joining us and please could he have my email address in order to send me the list of requirements. They would fund their own flight costs but would I sort out the accommodation and ground transport. He then stated his email address.

I replied immediately, to confirm that I had spoken to Mac and that I would sort out my visa application soonest.

If they needed an address to stay at for their application, I would be able to supply one.

The list of requirements arrived later that day, nothing too surprising on it, so Mac wouldn't be tasked too heavily.

I decided to add a few extras that I thought might be needed given the terrain and the likely weather.

Happy with what I hoped would cover all eventualities, I emailed it to Mac with a covering note that if he could think of anything that we hadn't, please add to the list and that I would sort out the bill with him later.

An email arrived in my inbox as I was sending my one to Mac, opening it after mine had gone I found that it was a request from Nick and Lisa for the address that we would be 'staying at'.

I typed out another email to Mac to request the address ASAP, adding it's for their visa application forms and is needed urgently as time is short.

Mac came straight back with the info and suggested that as the address was actually registered as a commercial enterprise, it might be best for everyone to apply for a 'Business' visa.

He had been giving the matter some thought and was of the opinion that as his business was 'Geological' in nature,

"We drill through rock and such searching for water," he wrote, "I will write a letter inviting you all out to view the drilling method, examine the rock tailings and debris, I'll make it sound official anyway."

"Sounds good to me," I wrote back, "I'll pass it on to Nick and Lisa, it'll cost them more for a business visa though but it might help given the address for sure.

I won't need to be mentioned on the letter, I'll come out as a tourist visiting my old friends, and with all the old visa stamps in my passport the authorities might think it strange if I am invited to view your methods given that I have been drilling for you for years."

Nick and Lisa were happy with the arrangements and with a copy of Mac's Letter of Invitation, attached to their visa application they sent the emails to the High Commission.

I had also emailed mine.

All we could do now was wait and hope.

The 'High Commission' was on form and true to the information on their website, we all had the request for our passports to be sent in, along with the relevant fees and self-addressed envelopes, of course.

We were 'Go for launch' as they say at 'NASA', Easter in Mozambique. We booked return flights individually, although we would travel as a group, with a ten-day period between them. We had decided that although that was probably much longer than was needed, it was better to spend a few days out there kicking our heels rather than running out of time.

Chapter 14

It was a long journey, not just in distance but in time as well, eleven hours to 'Johannesburg' two plus hours in the terminal and then another three to 'Nampula'.

By the time we had gotten through immigration, retrieved our baggage which unfortunately had to go in the aircraft's hold on the 'Nampula' leg due to the size of the aircraft used, cleared customs and emerged out into the bright sunlight of the day, we had been travelling for over twenty hours.

Thankfully, Mac had arranged for a driver to pick us up. A tall skinny African dressed in a flowery shirt and baggy jeans was dutifully holding up a large card with my name on it.

Talking fast and excitedly, he led us to a beaten-up but perfectly clean minibus, opening the sliding side door he ushered us in while he loaded our bags, seemingly puzzled as to why our bags were so light.

He slid the side door shut with gusto and then climbed into the driver's seat and started the engine.

Cooled air was soon wafting from the vents onto our sweaty faces, sheer bliss.

He turned to us, flashing a smile, "OK, boss, we go?"

"Yes," I said, "we go."

Despite the bumpy ride, we all slept sporadically during the drive to the 'Life Source' compound.

As we drove into the compound, Mac appeared in the doorway of his office and strode purposefully over to the minibus, opening the sliding door and beaming in.

"I bloody knew you would be back," he said, grasping my hand as I emerged from the vehicle.

"Yes, I know but I'm not staying for long."

As the others alighted from the minibus, I introduced them.

"Mac, this is Professor McLaren, she's our Geologist."

Mac was the most gracious I had ever seen him be.

"Professor, I am very pleased to meet you, if there is anything that you need, you only have to ask," then looking at me he said, "I would just like to add that anything my ex-employee has said to you about me is probably untrue." He grinned and looked her in the eye.

"Please call me Lisa," she said, "Martin has appraised us of your demeanour and so far, I think he was telling the truth." she grinned back.

"Ouch!"

Mac then turned to Nick.

"Dr Trulade or Nick?" he asked.

"Nick is fine."

"Tell me Nick," he continued, "is the professor's bark worse than her bite?"

"Oh, hell yes, don't rub her up the wrong way! I've never known her lose an argument yet."

The driver handed us our bags and was last seen heading out of the compound, leaving a trail of dust in his wake.

"Right, why don't I show you to your rooms and then we can relax with a beer or two.

I have reserved one for Lisa but you two blokes will have to share, hope that's OK?"

"Fine by me." said Nick.

"And by me," I agreed, "After all it's only for tonight, from then on we'll all be in one place anyway."

The evening passed peacefully, we drank very little, mainly because we were all knackered, sleep was just a nod away. So, after an hour or so polite conversation ceased and we crept to our rooms.

I could hear a knocking noise, rousing me from my slumbers, followed by someone shouting,

"Come on you lazy sod, it's nearly lunchtime."

I sat up and looked at my watch.

"Lunchtime, what's he on about, it's only 6:30."

Nick was sitting up, rubbing his eyes, "Is he always like that?" he asked.

"That's more like the Mac I know, last night's charm offensive was for Lisa's benefit I suspect."

After a breakfast fit for a king, we were presented with the gear that Mac had purchased on our behalf. Lisa methodically checked off each item as Nick and I placed them into three respective piles.

"What are these for?" She asked, holding up one of the short-handled mattocks that Mac had provided in the place of the 'Ice Axes' that I had requested.

"Well," Mac began, "your colleague here," he said pointing to me, "requested bloody 'Ice Axes' and those are the nearest things like it that I could find, I ask you 'Ice Axes' here in the middle of bloody Africa!"

They all looked at me, enquiringly.

"Well, given that the wet season has only just ended, the waterfall at the cave entrance may be in flood making it very difficult to gain entrance to the cave, so what I propose is that we enter the cave using the route that Jo and I used to get out, the only problem with that is that to access that entrance, we will have to climb a steep slope of loose rocks and scree. I thought that an ice axe or something similar would assist us in doing that and given that those mattocks have a spiked side as well as a blade, I think they will work perfectly."

Mac, beaming from ear to ear just said, "More of that bloody bullshit."

Lisa then picked up one of the crow bars, looked at me and said, "And these, are we going burgling?"

"No, the entrance is covered by a large flat stone, we will need to pry it up to gain access to the tunnel."

By the time we had finished checking and packing, it was early afternoon too late to attempt to drive to our drop-off point at the bottom of the ridge below our designated entry point.

I wasn't even sure where it was, I had surveyed the area below us when Jo and I came out of the tunnel and we had trekked at roughly 125 degrees according to the compass after descending the treacherous slope until we came to the road.

We decided that our best option was to leave at first light, Mac would drive us as far as possible to the base of the slope where we would then camp for the night and hopefully ascend the slope before the heat of the day took its toll on us.

First light, 04:30, it was refreshingly cool but as the sun rose we could feel its heat burning through. It took nearly five hours of tarmac driving to reach the area where I thought Jo and I had stepped on to the road. The vegetation had grown so much during the rains that I made Mac drive up and down the area a couple of times before I was sure that it was the right place.

"Any more of this pissing about," he said, "and I'll throw you out and go home!"

He turned off the road and followed the on-board compass heading of 305 degrees, after two hours of painfully slow progress we could see the ground rising in the distance, shimmering in the haze a mass rose out of the lush grass that had grown since the rain had started.

Another three hours and we could clearly see the scree-covered slopes. Mac drove to a flat area that was within one hundred metres of the base of the slope. Stopping the vehicle he said,

"That's it guys, you're on your own from now, I need to get back before it gets dark."

We got out, stretched our legs and unloaded the gear. Mac handed me a Sat-phone saying,

"Only use it when necessary, these things cost a fortune to use and don't bloody lose it."

"I won't," I replied.

He stepped closer, put his hand into his pocket and pulled out the 'Makarov',

"Here," he said, "just in case you run into trouble and it's in full working order, not like when you gave it to me."

He climbed back into the vehicle, shouted at Nick and Lisa to be careful and drove off the way we had come from.

I placed the loaded pistol into my rucksack, back where it had previously been kept. If Nick and Lisa had seen Mac give it to me, they showed no signs.

It was hot, the sun was baking the ground and turning the excess moisture into steam, it was like being in a sauna. There was no way that we should attempt to climb the slope today.

We looked for a suitable spot to make camp and settled on an area close to a clump of bushes, it would give us some protection from predators.

We stretched a light flysheet over a framework of thin carbon fibre poles and anchored it down with steel pegs and assorted rocks.

We ate a light meal of biscuits and cheese, washed down with water. The MRE's that we had brought with us needed hot water and we didn't want to light a fire.

Leaving Lisa in the camp, Nick and I walked along the base of the slope to examine it for the best spot to climb up and also for me to look for signs of where Jo and I had previously come down.

It all looked remarkably difficult and the rains appeared to have washed away any tracks that we might have previously left.

Chapter 15

Despite liberal use of mosquito repellent and the burning of three 'mosquito' coils, we were still feasted upon during the night, we all awoke in the early light of dawn to find each other rather blotchy.

A breakfast of the remaining cheese, with biscuits and energy bars and we were ready for the day.

We fastened a rope by means of a carabineer to each of our waists, the idea being that if one of us slipped, the other two of us could stop the slide.

With our rucksacks firmly strapped to our backs, we began the ascent, in single file initially with me leading followed by Lisa then Nick but after a while, it became apparent that that was fraught with danger, almost every step up the slope sent a shower of loose rocks to the person below, so we changed to a staggered line abreast. We could still stop one of us falling but at least we weren't splattering them with debris.

It took just over two and a half hours of hard climbing; our mattock points being thrust into the loose surface with each step to aid traction to reach the ridge line.

We sat on the edge of the ridge panting heavily with exertion, sweat pouring from our bodies soaking our clothing, looking not only down at the treacherous slope that we had just climbed but also at the vista before us.

We gulped down water from our bottles in an effort to quench our thirsts and took time to assess our situation.

I studied the horizon for points of reference and then looked along the ridge on my right, it seemed to me that we had climbed up to the ridge further to the left than where Jo and I had descended but it was definitely the same ridge.

We gathered ourselves and our gear. Still roped together, we made our way in single file towards the tunnel entrance. Yes, this was definitely the right place. I hadn't taken too much notice of the area when I had previously walked along the ridge, I was just looking for a way down but my memory seemed to have taken it on board.

Eventually I stopped, released myself from the rope and removed my rucksack.

"What's the matter?" Lisa asked, looking concerned.

"Nothing," I replied, "we are here!"

They both looked around.

"What's here?" They said in unison.

"The entrance!" I said pointing to a flat-topped stone that lay within a rocky outcrop.

"That's the flat stone that I mentioned, time to get out the crow bars."

Lisa looked at the flat stone with the interested eye of a professional. Brushing away accumulated dirt and debris and running her hands around the circumference she said,

"This rock is not of the same material as those around it and it has been worked to this shape, if you look carefully you can see ancient marks where someone has knapped it into shape to fit this recess."

We cleared away the remaining debris from the area around the stone's edge but still had to resort to chipping off the edge of the flat stone in order to get a purchase for the crow bars to prise it up, unfortunately erasing some of the 'Knappers' handiwork in the process. Slowly and with the aid of a mattock blade we inched the stone upward, a cool refreshing breeze exited the dark recess as we did so.

"Wow, you would not have known that was there." said Nick.

"I guess that was the general idea."

We propped the stone up by jamming two of the mattocks against its lower surface. That would allow us to close it down once we were inside in order to keep any intruders (animal or otherwise out).

I briefly explained the layout of the tunnel, not forgetting the loose rock traps that Jo and I had previously set.

We removed our headlamps from our rucksacks and clipped them onto our hard hats. We would only don the hats and switch the lamps on once in the tunnel.

We decided that Nick would be first to go into the tunnel, he would take the gear from us on the outside and stow it further down away from the entrance, Lisa and I would then follow. I would then close the entrance.

With Lisa's help by removing the mattocks while I held the weight of the stone, I sealed us in, gently lowering the stone once more into its recess.

With our 'headlamps' shining brightly, we could see the marks made by those who had painstakingly dug the tunnel many, possibly thousands of years ago.

We carried our gear in our hands, carefully dodging the traps as Nick, who was also using his handheld lamp, called them out.

Moving my head, I swept the light of my lamp across the left side of the tunnel roof as we descended, looking for the outlet of the air that had blown the flame of my torch when Jo and I had last descended the tunnel. I called to Lisa and Nick when I found it.

"Hey guys, I found this outlet on my previous visit but didn't get a chance to explore it. It is man-made but quite small and cool air flows from it. Something to investigate later perhaps?"

We continued on, further down the tunnel, a noise that I had not previously heard became apparent, becoming louder with every step towards the cave, a rumbling, roaring noise.

Cautiously, we stepped out into the main tunnel that connected the cave entrance to the large cave, there were no signs of life but the noise was even louder, not unbearable, just loud.

"OK," I said, "if we go that way," pointing to my left, "we will enter the big cave with the paintings or that way," pointing to my right, "to the waterfall."

They decided that the big cave was what they wanted to see first.

With Nick's hand-lamp lighting the way, I turned off my headlamp, no sense wasting the battery.

Paintings in that tunnel that Jo and I had seen before with the gloom of my wind-up torch now seemed more alive, the colours more vibrant but when we entered the large cave or cavern as it should be called, I was told by Lisa, our breath was taken away.

"Oh My God!" Nick and Lisa exclaimed.

"This is fantastic!"

"Truly amazing!"

Nick was moving his lamp around the walls, hovering on each painting for a short while before moving on to the next.

Lisa was rummaging in her rucksack for her own lamp.

I just stood there, grinning.

When eventually they turned and looked at me, I just said. "Do you believe me now?"

As an archaeologist, Nick was in his element, his enthusiasm for what was in front of his eyes was obvious, he was babbling incoherently and moving his arms and hands in sweeping movements as if conducting an orchestra.

I looked at Lisa, "Is he always like this?" I asked.

She shrugged her shoulders and said, "Truth is I don't know, I've never been on an expedition with him before."

Nick eventually turned towards us, tears in his eyes. "So beautiful, what a find," was all he could say.

"Right, well I don't know about you two but I think we should go to the front of the cave, sort ourselves out and make a cuppa, I'm parched."

As we made our way towards the cave entrance, the roaring noise got louder. I suddenly realised what it probably was.

"It's the waterfall," I said, "it's in flood, I guess after the rains, it must be under huge pressure coming out of that hole in the rock.

It was a good job we didn't try to get in that way."

The noise as we entered the passageway was deafening after the muted sound of the cavern, getting louder as we approached the cave mouth.

Nick moved his lamp from side to side as we walked, halting at each painting for a few seconds and enthusing over their beauty before moving on. We waited patiently while he did so, not just in politeness but also because he was in danger of running out of battery power for his lamp before he finished his exploration.

The wall of water was a magnificent sight, glowing bright silver, shot through with colour from the glare of the sunlight.

So great was the flow, that whereas before the water ran directly down the face of the cave entrance it now arched out over the pool like a large iridescent bubble, its outer edge a good two metres from the cave entrance but still encompassing the entrance totally.

Whilst Nick and Lisa stood entranced by the beauty of the falling water, I prepared to make a fire.

There was a little wood left from my previous stay in the cave and a few unburnt pieces left in the hearth, which I set aside while I rummaged to the bottom of my rucksack and withdrew a metal tin with a lid on it. It was oblong and had at some time probably held biscuits, now it held a small supply of charcoal and fire lighting sticks. (Items that I had requested Mac to obtain for me.)

Placing a 'firelighter' onto the hearth with some of the dry wood, I lit it with a match which had for obvious reasons been kept separately from the 'firelighters'.

When the fire was burning brightly, I added some of the charcoal; all I needed now was some water and I knew where I could get some.

From my rucksack, I pulled out a small flat pack bucket, a quick shake and it was ready for use, I picked up one of the ropes and was busy tying it around my waist when Lisa came into the alcove where I was standing.

She looked at me, "Thinking of going somewhere?" she asked.

"Oh no, just going to get some water, I thought I would tie myself to the rock in case I fall in, I wouldn't want to leave you alone at this stage of the game."

She smiled.

"OK, I'll hang on to the rope, we don't want to lose you either."

Bucket safely filled, I pumped some of the water out of it, through my purifier pump and into my mess tin, which I then placed on the hot stones of the hearth.

The water was soon boiling. There was enough water in the mess tin to use for three MREs and we each chose one from our supply.

I then boiled more water for tea and coffee.

It was quieter in the alcove, for some unknown reason the noise from the falling or should I perhaps more correctly say, gushing water seemed to bypass us and so we decided that given that there was ample room and a cosy fire we would after all camp there.

We ate our food as though we had never had anything so good, conversation was virtually non-existent until the last dregs of tea and coffee had gone.

We still had several hours of daylight left.

I posed a question to the others.

"Given the force of the water, might it be a better idea to finish what-ever you, looking at Nick, need to do before we venture out of the cave, just in case we can't get back in?"

"Sounds like a good idea," said Nick.

Lisa nodded in agreement.

"If we can help Nick to complete whatever he wants to do, we can all go out through the waterfall, if it's too difficult to get back into the cave, we can trek down through the forest to the grassland below, we've got a GPS, so I can call Mac with co-ordinates of where to pick us up when we come out."

We all agreed on that.

We carried Nick's equipment back down to the cavern and with the aid of mine and Lisa's hand-lamps, we lit a large area at a time of where he wanted to work.

Nick photographed every wall-painting in sequence, beginning from the left as we entered the cavern, carefully noting on his sketch pad dimensions and colours of each and every one.

He kept Lisa and me busy with a very large tape measure, measuring distances from wall to wall, painting to painting and stone seat to stone seat, he was very meticulous in his requirements.

We discovered that around the outer edge of the cavern and spaced equally between the wall paintings, fires had been previously lit, presumably to highlight the paintings.

"It must have been a fantastic sight," Lisa mused, "the flickering flames would have made the animals look like they were moving."

"The stone seats and table must have been for some sort of tribal council," Nick announced, "that large seat was probably for the chieftain."

The cavern was roughly one hundred metres in diameter and about sixty metres high,

"It was a natural cavern not man-made," Lisa said as she examined the rock surface, "thousands of years old." she took some small samples for testing on her return to the UK.

At last, Nick declared that he had done as much as he could, for the moment and so could we move to the paintings in the tunnel.

I looked at my watch, it said 21:05.Stating the time, I suggested that perhaps we should call it a day.

"We can go back, get a drink and something to eat and finish the tunnel paintings tomorrow." Nick looked positively peeved but he agreed so we headed back to the fireside.

The fire had almost burnt out but with a little coaxing and the rest of the dry wood, it soon burst into life.

I boiled some more water and we once again dined on MREs washed down with coffee.

Washing ourselves posed a problem, not because we were shy but because the water at the mouth of the cave was no longer easily reachable.

We tied a rope around our waists and a suitable distance along the rope was tied off to a rocky protrusion in case we slipped, with the aid of my bucket, also suitably tied to rope, we managed one at a time to rinse ourselves of the day's grime. It's surprising just how much, cold running water can invigorate you.

With our sleeping mats laid out near to the fire and the sound of running water in our ears, we slept soundly.

Dawn had broken when I woke up. Looking around, I saw Lisa still curled up on her mat. Nick however was nowhere to be seen. For a moment, panic set in.

"Oh god," I wondered, "has he fallen into the pool!" I got up to walk towards the cave mouth, as I did so, my eye registered movement down in the passage to the cavern, I could make out the light of one maybe two lamps shining on the wall and the profile of Nick busily scribbling onto his notepad. I heaved a sigh of relief.

I made up the fire, with another firelighter, charcoal and the still warm embers of last night's fire and in no time at all, the water was boiling for breakfast.

Lisa awoke while I was stirring my tea. I offered her some, which she gladly accepted.

"Where's Nick?" she asked.

"Down there," I pointed, then explained that I had found him missing when I had woken up.

Lisa was looking around for something!

"What's up?" I asked her.

"I need to pee," she answered.

"OK, you see that little alcove by the left side of the waterfall? We used that when we were here last time, I'll take Nick some coffee and give you privacy, just don't fall in. It might be advisable to tie yourself to some rope," I added.

As I walked down the passageway with Nick's coffee in my hand, Lisa made her way to the alcove, I didn't hear any screams.

"Jesus Nick, you nearly gave me a heart attack," I said as I handed him his coffee. "I woke up and you were gone, I thought you'd fallen in the pool!"

"Sorry, I woke up early and just couldn't wait to get this done, it's so exciting, it's a dream come true."

"Well dream or not, you had me worried."

"Anyone for breakfast?" Lisa called as she walked towards us holding three silver packets with spoon handles poking out of the top.

We stood in front of possibly a two to three thousand-year-old painting of an ox type animal lit by the one of the lamps that Nick was using, eating a hot MRE from a foil packet.

"Surreal."

By the time that Nick had finished cataloguing his 'artefacts' as he called them, it was nearly midday. He was particularly enthusiastic about the brush lights, which he told me with great delight were actually made of reeds and bound with brushwood.

"The workmanship and attention to detail is wonderful," he declared, "the actual torch section appears to be coated in a mix of what is probably animal fat and beeswax. They must have burnt for ages."

"They did," I said, "we used a few when we explored."

Both Nick and Lisa looked at me in horror.

I just shrugged, "We needed the light," I said, "but we did leave some."

We estimated that it would take at least one hour to pack and waterproof our packs and prepare ourselves to leave the cave, actually getting ourselves and our gear to the other side of the pool would probably take another forty-five minutes to an hour, which meant that it would be dark before we were ready to move on, providing that Lisa had satisfied her curiosity regarding the 'whirlpool' so we decided that we would stay another night in the cave rather than camp in the forest with the attendant mosquitoes and other biting creatures for company.

We spent the afternoon examining the cave, cavern and both tunnels for any previously missed 'Archaeological' artefacts and any other clues to the previous occupants other than Jo and myself.

Nick wanted to concentrate on the paintings, Lisa and I decided to investigate the small tunnel within the one that we had entered the cave through and it proved to be just as surprising as the paintings.

Lisa and I retraced our steps towards our entry point until we reached the opening high in the tunnel sidewall, it was just big enough for a small person to enter.

"I'll go," said Lisa, "no disrespect but you might miss something."

"That's fine, I'll wait here for you, might be a good idea to tie a rope around yourself in case you get into trouble, I can at least try to pull you out."

"OK, sounds like a plan, I'll need a help up into it and then pay the rope out as I go in, and I'll shout and pull on the rope if I need help."

I could hear only the scrape of boots and laboured breathing as Lisa slowly inched forward. It seemed an eternity before I heard a muffled voice telling me that she was coming out. I gathered the rope in as Lisa eased towards me, eventually her boots followed by the rest of her eased out of the opening.

I shone the torch on her face to be greeted with a large smile. Then I burst out laughing.

"What's wrong?" Lisa asked.

"If only you could see yourself, apart from your sparkly green eyes and your perfectly white teeth, you are totally black; you look like a chimney sweep's lad."

"That's because I have just come out of a chimney!"

"Pardon?"

"This tunnel is a chimney, it goes all the way down to the roof of the cavern, presumably to allow smoke to exit, I could hear Nick talking to himself about the paintings, actually he was probably talking into his recorder and I could see light from his hand-lamp. I guess if he had looked up he would have seen light from my headlamp dancing around in the darkness."

"So we are standing in a chimney?"

"From here on up, yes, I would say so but down to the main tunnel, I would say was an entry/exit, maybe even an escape tunnel. Whoever used this cavern certainly had some advanced ideas."

"Right, what I really need is a shower, any chance you could oblige with the bucket?"

Having washed away the soot from herself and her clothes, Lisa stood by the fire to dry herself, that was when she noticed the neatly folded clothes that Jo had left on the rock ledge, she smiled and said to herself,

"Ah, a woman's touch obviously."

However, they were the only artefacts that we found.

Chapter 16

We were awake before dawn, I boiled water one last time on our little fire, carefully using only enough charcoal for our needs; I reckoned that we might need the rest when we exited the forest.

We packed our rucksacks leaving just the ropes to hand, we had also stripped to our underwear and packed our clothes, we would get soaked going through the waterfall and it would be best to be able to put on dry clothes after.

Anticipating this way out of the cave, I had ordered three large, strong plastic sacks and tie-wraps on my list to Mac, he hadn't let me down.

We stuffed the rucksacks into individual bags and sealed them with a tie-wrap, the next problem was how to tie them securely enough to be able to get them through the waterfall and across the whirlpool without losing them.

Nick came to the rescue.

"No problem," he said, "I'm an old hand at securing precious loads," and he proceeded to wrap the first one. "There, that won't come undone," he declared.

"It looks good enough but we really need to string the three in a line, each about forty metres apart and with a long enough line in front to carry across the pool first." I said.

"OK, make this the last of the line, measure the distance to the next and I'll tie that off and then the next."

We were left with a line of about forty metres, just enough I hoped.

"Right, the plan is, I'll go first, I've done it before and so I know what I'm in for, you will need to keep your back as close to the wall as possible and work your way sideways, it may be slippery underfoot, so take it slowly.

I'll have this rope around my waist, which I would like you to feed out as I go, these knots should help you pull me in if I fall. If I don't make it, leave by the way we entered.

When I reach the other side of the pool, I will give two tugs on the rope. I want you to tie your end to Lisa and as she comes across, I'll pull it in.

We'll tie this other rope with the packs on to Lisa as well and then Nick, if you feed it out as she comes across, we'll both have her if she slips. Once she's on dry land, I can assist you. So if you tie yourself to a rope and attach the other end to the last pack with about twenty metres or so, then once I've pulled the packs over, Lisa and I will be ready for you."

We set about putting knots in the ropes at about two metre intervals, it may not have been necessary but it would help if we had to pull one of us out of the whirlpool's grip.

Satisfied that we all understood the plan and that we were all suitably tied to each other, I ventured out into the torrent of remarkably cold water. The force of it tried to wash me off the ledge, had I been wearing my rucksack it most definitely would have done so. I was through, I gingerly made my way along the ledge, Nick paying out the rope as I moved along and then, 'terrafirma', although it was difficult to decide initially where the poolside was, so great was the flow from the fissure in the rock that the pool was overflowing, no longer the steady trickle that I had seen on my last visit.

I gave two tugs on the rope and waited. The rope started to slacken off and I began to take in the slack, slowly hand over hand, the water at the edge of the waterfall started to fly in all directions and Lisa, clad only in a hard hat and underwear slowly emerged, gasping for breath as she did so, her hair that hung outside of her hat plastered to her face, her concentration was visibly apparent.

"OK, you're doing fine," I called, "We've got you."

She slowly and carefully worked her way around and virtually fell into my arms as she reached the safety of land.

"I've never been so frightened," she said, "but it was also exhilarating at the same time," a broad smile across her face.

I undid the rope from her that held the packs, I didn't want to risk her being dragged into the whirlpool in the event that something went wrong.

Two tugs and then we heaved, the first pack was in the water, we stood to the side of the pool hoping to avoid the centre of the vortex which would be where it would be strongest, whether it made any difference I don't know, it was hard work, thank goodness for the knots, as soon as the first pack was on dry ground, the second hit the water, again we heaved and then again for the third.

"I hope we don't have to pull Nick out," Lisa said, "I'm knackered."

"Me too," I replied.

Two tugs, take up the slack and then Nick grinning as he emerged from his cold shower, carefully working his way around to safety.

"What a buzz!" was all he could say when he reached us.

We stood a little way back from the poolside, the overflow lapping our feet before disappearing into the undergrowth.

"I think we should find a dry spot and get some clothes on," Lisa said, "I would hate to be seen like this, my undies are totally see through, people might get the wrong idea!"

"And the mosquitoes will have a feast," I added.

We moved slightly up hill to the left side of the pool to where Jo and I had camped that first night last November. We undid the rope from our packs and struggled to remove the tie-wraps from the plastic bags that we had placed the rucksacks in, in the end we gave up, I tore my bag open and with access to my rucksack I pulled out my knife and cut the tie-wraps on the other packs.

We dried ourselves as best we could but with the temperature and humidity rising, it was an uphill task to stay dry; by the time we had dressed, we were damp with perspiration.

Lisa now had the chance to investigate the mysterious 'Whirlpool' or 'Vortex' as it was more correctly called.

She decided that the best way to view it would be from up high and so she started to climb to the cliff edge above the waterfall.

Concerned that she might slip and fall into the pool, I insisted that she tie a rope around herself and that either I or Nick be on hand to hold it.

"On second thoughts," I said, "I think it might be better to loop the rope around a tree as well, that way if you fall you won't pull whichever one of us is on the other end in as well."

Nick volunteered to be the safety man. I decided that he was definitely an adrenaline junkie.

They worked their way around the cliff edge from one side to the other.

While they were working their way around the pool, I checked the 'Makarov', cleaning it as best I could before slipping it into my waist band.

Finally, Lisa had seen all that she could,

"It's no good," she announced as they came back to where I was sitting, "there's too much water flowing, I guess I need to come back in a month or so."

"You must have some ideas though?" I asked.

"Yes, I would speculate that the rock formation below and around us is riddled with fissures, holes if you like and that the cave probably extended further out than at present. The rock in this part of the country is mainly 'Pre Cambrian' and consists of many sub types, some softer than others. Over time, water has flowed from way up the hill through possibly many fissures and formed what is now that outlet. That flow has eroded the rock here, consequence being that it has eaten through to another fissure below us into which it now flows.

The 'Vortex' effect is possibly due to a choking of the flow either because of debris that has fallen into the hole or because the fissure or fissures that it is flowing into cannot cope with the flow."

"But what about the gurgling noise and the fall and rise of the water level that Jo and I saw?"

"That could be due perhaps to some material in the hole moving and temporarily blocking the outlet, some vegetation, or animal perhaps? The pressure would soon push it either out of the way or simply down further. A bit like when the sink waste gets clogged."

We had spent over three hours inspecting the pool and we needed to get out of the forest and make camp before nightfall.

Nick noticed the pistol.

"Where did that come from?" He asked, "And why do you have it tucked in to your trousers?"

"It's a long story. I gave it to Mac when I left originally, he gave it back to me when he dropped us off, in case we needed a little protection. We didn't need it in the cave but out here and going down through the forest, I thought it safer to have it to hand, even if I only use it to scare animals away."

It took a little over three hours to reach the edge of the forest to where the now lush grass was growing, we hadn't pushed too hard, we had stopped on the way to pick some fruit, which we ate as we walked but it was tough going, everything that could, seemed to want to bite us, the mosquito repellent was almost useless.

Reaching the grassland was a relief. We took a left turn, the intention, I explained was that this was the way that Jo and I had been travelling when we smelled the smoke and then the sounds of the militia and why we had then gone into the forest.

The militia had subsequently been eliminated according to 'Coronel Almeida' and so it should be safe. Not only that, it was also the way to a village that the militia had previously raided and would be a good place to camp for night, I added that I would call Mac when we get there and arrange for a pick-up in the morning.

We had been walking for some while not really talking a lot just admiring the view, seeing the occasional animal, usually as it bounded away in alarm when an oily, sickly, nauseating smell became apparent, the further along our intended path the stronger it got, there was even a tinge of burning to it.

Our horror at what we found could not be imagined, an area of blackened earth through which new growth was pushing through was surrounded by the burnt remains of native huts and burnt vehicles. The foliage, once blackened by fire, was also growing anew but it was what was in the centre of the village, on what presumably had been the militia's parade ground that was not only the cause of the smell but also the greatest horror.

A partially dismantled pile of twisted limbs and burned blackened bodies was to be seen, Iridescent trails of unburnt diesel leached from beneath. As I ventured nearer, stepping over and around half-eaten body parts, my hand over my mouth, a cloud of fat black flies rose angrily from the stinking pile, rats alarmed at the sound of footsteps also ran out in all directions. I heard a retching sound from behind me and turned to see Lisa doubled over, vomiting forcefully into the blackened dust, Nick just staring in horror at the mass.

To one side of the mound of rotting corpses, atop a pole of about two metres high, a human head looked towards the grisly mass.

It was a large head, undoubtedly formerly belonging to a bull of a man. Flies took to the air in alarm as I approached, creating the effect of a black veil being lifted in order to reveal the full horror underneath.

Tendrils of rotting flesh hung precariously from the skull, squirming maggots fighting for the remaining morsels, some falling from the empty eye sockets and gaping mouth to lay in the sticky dust at the base of the pole.

Despite the horror before my eyes, I felt no revulsion and no pity; a proverb, impressed upon my younger self countless years ago by the 'Pastor' at Sunday school came to mind.

"We reap what we sow."

I turned away and re-joined Nick and Lisa.

When Lisa eventually regained her composure and after rinsing her mouth with water she said,

"My god! This is beyond belief, it's a war crime surely. We must report this to the authorities at once."

"A crime, yes. A war crime? No, this is African justice."

"What do you mean!" Exclaimed Lisa, "African justice? It's mass murder."

"These people," I said, pointing to the heap of very dead humanity, "have paid the ultimate price.

What has happened to them is no worse than what they did to countless innocent villagers, indeed it is probably less bad than what they did.

These were the very people who raided the village that I managed to escape from. They roared in on those trucks, shooting men, women and children dead and they were the more fortunate ones.

Many women were brutally raped before being thrown onto the dust and then killed.

Adolescents were rounded up and taken away, for what I don't know, I can only guess.

Jo was raped by several men and left to die in a hut, I managed to rescue her before these bastards came along and set the hut that she was in on fire, thankfully they didn't bother to check that she was still in it. The rest of her team and mine were also murdered by these bastards."

"Do I condone what has happened here? No, but I don't disapprove of it either.

I am partially responsible for what happened here, I was unaware of what actually took place but I pointed out the approximate position of this camp to the 'Coronel'. I was informed later that the camp had been found and the occupants and the camp had been eliminated."

"We westerners tend to look at the rest of the world in the way that we live and that, in many respects is wrong, each culture has its own set of rules and ideals. What you and I think of as barbaric are a normal way of life for many people, it is our interference in many cases that causes so much trouble.

If in the UK for instance, a gang of murderers killed a large amount of people. When and if the police caught them, what would happen?

I'll tell you, the 'do-gooder gang' would get involved, claiming that the miscreants or at least some of them had had an unfortunate upbringing or such and had subsequently lost their way in life, that they needed rehabilitation.

The leaders of the gang might get life in jail, which, in real time means about fifteen years, then they would be out and most likely re-offend, maybe even kill again.

Here, they've paid the ultimate price, they will never re-offend and that will probably save countless lives."

Lisa had removed her backpack and was pulling a thick black strap out of the top of it.

"No photos!" I shouted.

"But this needs to be documented," she said, "someone needs to be held accountable for this."

"Lisa! Listen to me. You obviously haven't understood a word of what I have just been saying.

This concerns you as well, Nick. African governments, as well as many others are paranoid about security, they like to keep as much under wraps as possible.

You may have noticed the long queues waiting at the security gate at the airport when we arrived here. They are especially thorough on people who are leaving the country, even more so foreigners.

It would only take one particularly zealous guard to check your camera and the pictures on it and you would be in deep shit and that would also include anyone travelling with you.

Pictures of a waterfall, caves and even the paintings in them you would probably get away with, but pictures of this," I said pointing towards the burnt huts and vehicles, "and especially of the pile of bodies would at the very least earn us all a very unpleasant time being questioned and probably incarcerated.

Not only that, Mac would be drawn into the fracas, he after all wrote the letter of invitation to you both that helped with your 'visa' applications.

Even if by some miracle the authorities let you off with a warning, which I doubt, you would never be allowed back to continue exploring.

It's just not worth the risk!

Now, I think it's time that we made a move."

We followed what remained of the vehicle tracks towards what I hoped would be the burnt-out village that I had seen on the photos in Greenlove's office.

The vegetation with the help of the rain had grown quickly and thickly to obscure much of the area and we relied on the more obvious signs such as broken branches to indicate the route.

Finally as the sun was beginning to set we emerged from the canopy, I could understand why the 'Coronel's' men had not been able to find the militia earlier.

The village had been totally destroyed by the militia and presumably, the villagers had also suffered the same fate.

We set up camp at the far end of what was the village, away from the forest where the insects were in abundance.

With a fire burning brightly, mosquito coils wafting their fragrant smoke into the air we ate and drank hot coffee.

I took a reading from Lisa's GPS and powered up the Sat-phone. It took several minutes to boot up and lock on to a signal but with a 'Green' light, it was good to go.

Mac had thoughtfully taped his number onto the casing of the handset, not that I had forgotten it but was in case I was incapacitated and Nick or Lisa needed to use it.

It took a while to connect, emitting weird noises during the process but eventually Mac answered.

"Still with us then!" He said.

"Oh yes but we will need picking up in a different place to where we were dropped off, I won't bore you with the details. If you have a pen and paper, I've got the GPS co-ordinates."

"Huh, give you an inch and you take a bloody mile, OK, go ahead."

I think Mac must have been punching the Lat/Long into his computer as I read the numbers to him, he simply said.

"Bit closer than the drop-off, can be there before lunch. That OK?"

"Brilliant, see you then and thanks."

We sat around the fire long into the night talking about the next steps that Nick and Lisa would take on their return to the UK, how they would approach their respective university governors with the evidence of their finds.

I was quite happy for them to take the credit. It had been mine and Jo's good luck to find the cave in the first place, it had very probably saved our lives and that for me was enough.

They both told me that they would ensure that in their reports they would make it clear that the 'Find' had been brought to their attention by a couple who had stumbled (their words) upon it during a wildlife adventure.

How could I disagree with that?

Eventually, tiredness set in, so I stoked up the fire with enough wood to burn through until dawn and joined the others under the flysheet for a few hours of hopefully peaceful sleep.

A night in the African bush is never really quiet. It is the time when the predators are most active. Noises, some of them blood-curdling in nature are quite frequent but with the fire burning brightly, the only creatures that got to us were the mosquitoes, again.

Chapter 17

Morning arrived, the sunrise setting the sky ablaze with colour, streaks of wispy white cloud interwoven with the beams of brilliant orange and pink against the Azure blue. The promise of another hot day.

True to his word, Mac arrived before lunch and to our delight, he brought lunch with him.

"Our first truly cold drink in days and sandwiches."

We had spent the morning while waiting for Mac pottering around the village and the immediate area. Lisa had taken some photos of the scenery, carefully ensuring that the destruction of the village was not shown, it seemed that my little outburst had hit home. Nick was just happy looking for, as he put, anything of interest.

The journey back was indeed shorter and much quicker. We ate and drank as Mac drove.

About an hour into the journey, I recognised the place where I had made the driver stop the 4x4 and where I had shot him after he threatened Jo and was intent on killing me. Thankfully, there were no bodies to be seen. It had been several months back. I said nothing about it to my travelling companions, best left that way.

We arrived at the compound as nightfall was setting in, to my delight some of my old colleagues were back at base, having completed another successful drill, the beer and tall tales flowed well into the early hours. Lisa retired early, muttering something about 'too much testosterone' for her liking, Mac simply slipped away sometime later.

Sleeping arrangements had changed, Lisa still had a room to herself but Nick and I had to bunk down in the crew room, no problem, we basically just stopped drinking, rolled over on the floor and fell asleep, the other guys switched the lights off on the way out.

Morning came around too quickly, my head was throbbing and my mouth was like the bottom of a parrot's cage, Nick declared that he wasn't much better off either.

The problem was, that sleeping in the crew room meant that it was a hive of activity at that time of the morning and apart from the noise, we were in danger of being trodden on.

We still had two days before our flights home and so at Mac's suggestion, we followed the team to their next drilling site, to gain as Mac said 'irrefutable evidence' that Nick and Lisa had been involved in the activities as outlined in his letters regarding the visa applications.

Whether Nick or Lisa realised the sheer hard work that was involved, I do not know but they knuckled down and helped out with the initial setting up of the equipment before finding reasons to 'explore the surroundings', although Lisa did examine the soil and rock deposits that the drill bit was extracting.

The villagers were most interested in the fact that a woman was working with us and many sat and watched her as she carefully and slowly picked through the deposits. Probably thinking that she was crazy!

We were staying that night at the village and after showering under a perforated bucket and changing into some clean clothes, we were treated to a celebratory meal by the villagers as a reward for finding the water.

African hospitality can be a long and colourful affair and so it was well after sunset before we finally and gratefully made it to our beds.

After a light breakfast, we bade farewell to the team, who still had work to do at the drill site and to the village Chieftain, before climbing aboard the truck for the final trip to the compound.

We had a flight scheduled for early the following day and Mac had arranged for a driver to take us to the airport later in the day, that would allow us to stop in a hotel that he had also arranged for the night in order to 'freshen up' he said.

"Can't have you going home looking and smelling like a bunch of vagrants."

We said our good-byes, Lisa giving Mac a rather long and over-friendly hug whispering something in his ear, to which he smiled broadly. Nick and I just shook his hand.

I had previously left the Makarov with him and it was now safely locked away in his safe.

"Have a safe trip, you Pommie bastard," he shouted to me as we drove out of the compound, "I'll put the bill in the post." a huge grin on his face.

It felt strange, sitting in a hotel lounge, sipping a glass of wine, soft music wafting through the speaker system while attentive waiters were hovering in the background, ready to assist at the raising of a hand, a far cry from the antics of the last few days.

Talk was of how the find would progress, of the processes and hurdles that Nick and Lisa would need to navigate in order to not only gain financial backing for an expedition to take place but also the various permissions and encumbrances that would require careful attention.

We arrived at the airport with several hours to spare, if the check-in queue seemed long, it was nothing compared to the queue for security. Luckily for us, with only hand baggage we were only given a cursory search.

Several hours later and after a quick trip around the duty-free shops at Johannesburg Airport, we were sitting in our seats on a Jumbo bound for London.

After clearing immigration and customs at Heathrow, we said our good-byes. Nick and Lisa organised a hire car, whereas I had decided to take the train.

"I'll call you in a few days," Nick said, "and keep you in the loop with regards to what is happening."

"Thanks but it's over to you now. I'll be available if you need any info, of course but any exploring will be down to you and your teams.

I'm going to take it easy, enjoy life. Maybe take a holiday.

I have enjoyed our time together and am genuinely pleased to have met you both. I wish you both the best of luck and look forward to reading your books or papers on the find whenever they are published."

"I'm sure Mac will be only too pleased to help if he can," adding whilst looking at Lisa, "I reckon he's got a soft spot for you."

She blushed.

We parted in the arrival's hall, they going out to the 'Avis' pick-up point, me going for the underground.

Part 3

Chapter 18

Johann de Klerk was sitting on the stoep [8], a half-empty glass of ice cold beer on the table beside him. He was reading The Herald, when an article caught his attention.

"Anika," he called, a tall slim woman with golden hair came out of the house.

"Yes," she answered.

"Here, read this," Johann said as he placed a half-folded newspaper into her hands.

Under the heading of 'International News' was an article relating to a find of archaeological significance in Mozambique. A cave containing several exquisite paintings of long extinct animals and protected by a 'Wonder' of nature had been found and was being explored by a team from the Ministry of Culture and Tourism assisted by teams from the Universities of Winchester and Southampton in the UK.

The location was not disclosed due to the significance of the find and of the danger that it posed to the public at large.

Full details would be published in due course.

Anika let the newspaper droop in her hands, she looked at her husband of thirty-six years and as if by some strange unseen connection, they both said to each other,

"Johanna talked about a cave with paintings!"

"Should we tell her?" Anika asked her husband.

Johann looked at her. "Do you think that it might help? She is getting much stronger, perhaps this might help with the healing. If I remember correctly, the Doctor seemed to indicate that the time in the cave was a happy one!"

"We can tell her about it when she wakes up, she is having a middagslapie. [9]

---

[8] Verandah

[9] Afternoon nap

Johanna came out onto the stoep, stretching as she did so, and the afternoon breeze, hot and dry ruffled her hair.

Her parents were sitting on either side of the small table, so Johanna opted for the swinging hammock at the far end.

She noticed that her parents seemed a little pensive, as though they had something to tell her.

"What is the matter Ma?" She asked.

"Nothing," her mother answered, "Pa and I have something to show you but we are a little unsure if we are doing the right thing."

Johanna got up from the hammock, her interest piqued by what her mother had said and walked over to her parents.

Her mother picked up the newspaper, indicated the article and placed it in Johanna's hands. She watched, hardly daring to breathe as her daughter read and then reread the article.

She watched as tears formed in Johanna's eyes and began to roll down her cheeks.

"Our cave, they've found our cave!" She exclaimed, "I knew they would, I hope they look after it."

Her tears were flowing freely, not of sorrow but of joy.

Her parents, initially concerned that it had been a step too far could now see that they had been right to show her the article.

"Oh, it's wonderful, Ma, Pa, you should see it. Life-size or maybe bigger paintings adorn the walls, all in glorious colour and the 'Waterfall' where we washed and stayed safe." she stopped and re-collected her thoughts and memories, "Martin," she suddenly said, "I wonder if he knows, I wonder where he is? I wonder if he told someone about the Cave?"

"Well, why don't you ask him?" Her mother replied.

"I don't know where he is, I don't know where to start, it's been so long and I still don't remember everything. I try but my mind is blank, only my dreams seem real and most of them are bad."

"You could always try where you were stationed. That was where they sent you to Pretoria hospital from. Perhaps someone there will know something."

"Yes, perhaps I should, I will call them right away, if you think that it is the right thing to do."

"You must do what feels right to yourself," her father said, "if it feels right, it is right."

Leaving her parents staring in amazement at her reaction to the article, Johanna went to her bedroom and eagerly turned the pages of her notebook to find the telephone number of the medical centre in Marrupa.

She walked back into the lounge. Her parents were already there, standing by the phone.

"We are just here in case you need us." her mother said, as she handed Johanna the handset.

She dialled the number, it rang several times and then a cheerful female voice answered,

"Universal Medical, Karen speaking. How may I help you?"

"Hi Karen, its Johanna."

Silence for a few seconds.

"Johanna! Johanna de Klerk! Is that you?"

"Yes, yes, it's me."

"Oh my God. How are you? It's been so long. Where are you?"

Johanna could hear Karen telling everyone near to her that Johanna was on the phone.

"I'm good thanks, well, getting better anyway. I'm back at home with my parents.

I have to go to the hospital once a month to be analysed, all part of the healing process apparently but other than that I am doing OK."

Karen relayed it to others who had gathered around.

"I hope you don't might me asking," Johanna continued, "but I'm hoping that one of you might know where Martin, the guy who brought me in, is?"

"Oh, I guess you weren't aware, given your condition. Greenlove had you shipped out but wouldn't tell your Martin where you were going, it caused an argument, apparently Greenlove if I remember correctly, told him that because he was not your kin nor had you expressed a desire for him to be told, he was not allowed to be informed.

Your Martin apparently told Greenlove that we were right about him, that he was not a fully functioning human being, I only wish I had been there to see it."

Johanna laughed, the first time in a long time.

"Then he apparently left. No, he saw Dr Max and left a letter for you which I believe was put into the company mail sack."

"Is Max there?"

"No, he's up country, doing the rounds, back in a few days."

"OK, when he gets back can you tell him I called, maybe he can call me or better still email me."

"Sure thing, I guess we have it all on file."

"It used to be. Anyway, thanks for your help."

"That's OK, look after yourself and I'll let Max know that you called. Bye."

Johanna's parents had moved away from the telephone once they were satisfied that the conversation was not likely to cause any distress to their daughter and were once more sitting outside.

Johanna went out to find them and tell them what had been said, it was when she mentioned about the letter that her mother put her hand to her mouth,

"Oh my goodness, I have a letter, it came while you were in hospital, we didn't tell you then because you were in a bad way and we thought that it might upset you, then to be honest, I forgot all about it."

She hurried off into the house and came back a short while later, a brown envelope in her hand.

Johanna took the envelope from her mother's hand and opened it. Inside was a battered white envelope, her name was handwritten on it and it was marked 'Private'. Sent to the UMA head office and had then been redirected to her home.

She sat down and with trembling fingers opened the envelope and removed the letter. It was written on company notepaper, by hand.

She read it, not once, not twice but three times, tears flowing down her face and onto her flowery cotton dress.

Her mother concerned by what she saw came over and sat beside her daughter to comfort her.

"Is it bad?" she asked.

"Oh no," she sobbed, "not bad at all, not anymore." She passed the letter to her mother to read.

"You must send him an email straight away." She said to Johanna, passing the letter to her husband and then clasped her still sobbing daughter firmly in her arms.

"But what shall I write?" She asked her mother as she sat at her father's desk, the computer screen glowing brightly in front of her. "It's been such a long time, he's probably forgotten all about me. Maybe he thinks that I don't want to see him."

"That letter that you have just read would seem to me to indicate that he cared very much for you and if he is anything like the man that you have described to your Pa and me, then I think he would be only too glad to hear from you."

"But why has he not tried to find me?"

"Maybe he has. But obviously your former employer wouldn't help and South Africa is a big country. Did you tell him where you lived?"

"I don't know, I can't remember."

"Well then, it would be an almost impossible task I would think, de Klerk is a very common name, probably hundreds of families and who would he ask?"

"Yes, you are probably right."

Johanna logged in to her email account and typed maartin1065@hotmail.com into the address box.

Dear Martin,

I do not know where to start.

I have only just been given your letter.

My parents received it while I was in hospital and thought that it was best to wait until I was better before giving it to me to read.

You had marked it 'Private', so they didn't read it themselves.

It was only when I read of the discovery of 'our cave' in the newspaper that my memory was jogged into life.

I called UMA and asked if they knew where you were, Karen told me that you had written a letter to me and Max had put it in the company mail.

When I told Ma and Pa about the letter, Ma suddenly remembered the letter that had arrived all those months ago.

I am so glad to have received it and so sorry that Greenlove gave you grief.

I would love to see you or even just talk to you, if you prefer.

Love,
Jo.

She hit the send key and waited.

Johanna sat at her father's desk for a good thirty minutes, willing the computer to announce receipt of an email, nothing came.

Well, at least it didn't bounce back, she consoled herself but disappointment was setting in.

"Maybe he's at work," her mother told her, "it's still early in the day and if he's working in the bush, it might be days before he gets the email."

"Yes, I suppose you are right."

"Het geduld kind [10]

and come and help me make the dinner."

---

[10] Have patience child

Chapter 19

Martin parked the car in bay ten, his allocated parking place; opening the back door, he gathered his bags of groceries and pushed the door shut with his backside, a press of a button on the remote and he was on his way into the building.

His flat was on the second floor and with two flights of stairs to climb, he only ever bought small amounts of food at any one time, lugging several heavy bags up the stairs was not his idea of fun.

Entering his flat, he placed his purchases in their respective cupboards; he made a cup of tea and sat at his desk, initially just enjoying the view of the boats swaying gently at their moorings in the marina, the boat owners and countless holiday makers milling around enjoying the weather.

He looked at the clock, 19:20, just time to check for emails before the next episode of a TV drama that he had been watching.

He booted up his computer, tapped in the password and with everything online he selected email.

'Ping', he had three email messages, one of them caught his eye immediately.

'Karoogirljdk'

His heart was pounding, he had almost given up. He selected the box, milliseconds passed and then her email was there in front of him.

Dear Martin, he read, barely taking in what was in front of him, his mind racing to comprehend the moment, she hadn't forgotten him, it was just a delay, of no fault of hers.

He replied immediately.

Dear Jo,

I am overjoyed that not only have you replied to my letter but that you are also safe and well.

I was distraught when told by Mr Greenlove that you had been shipped out and even more annoyed when he wouldn't tell me where you were going. I'm afraid I lost my temper. Luckily for me, Max helped me out by allowing me to get a letter to you.

Given the time that has passed, I had almost given up hope of seeing or hearing from you again.

I travelled out to Mozambique last April with two university academics. I took them to our cave. They have been working there with the authorities for some time now.

There is too much to put on email but if you like, I will call your home phone if you give me the number.

Whatever else happens, stay safe.

Your fellow cave dweller,
Martin.

He hit send.

Ping! The computer on her father's desk announced an email. Johanna pounced on it and opened the mailbox.

"He's replied, Martin has answered," she shouted to her parents.

Sitting in her father's office chair, she read the email out loud to herself and answering the question to herself also,

"Of course you can have the number." she said.

"Ma, Pa, Martin would like to call me, it's OK to give him the number, isn't it?"

Her mother looked at her father, who shrugged his shoulders before answering,

"I do not think it will be a problem."

"Johanna," her mother said, "be careful, take your time and if you feel unsure about anything make your excuses, you can always call another day."

Jo was already typing an email,

Dear Martin,
Please call, I can't wait to hear from you.
Jo
+27 41 742691

She pressed send and waited.

Martin was sitting at his desk, all thoughts of the TV drama gone. He heard the 'Ping' and opened the email.

Writing the number down on his notepad to make sure he didn't lose it, he picked up the phone and dialled.

It was answered on the first ring.

"Martin?"

"Hi Jo, how are you?"

"Good. Really good now."

"It's been a while, so much has happened."

"Yes. I know. Well, I know some of it, there is a lot that I don't remember. Gaps in my memory, the doctors say that I might not remember everything."

"Well, you suffered pretty badly, some of it might be best not remembered but I will help where I can."

"Thanks, it's so good to hear your voice."

"And yours. I presume that you are living with your parents?"

"Yes, back on the farm. Ma and Pa are taking good care of me. I have to go to the hospital in Willowmore once a month, for a check-up, to be analysed is more like it.

But I don't go out anywhere on my own, I don't feel safe."

"I guess it will take time, you went through a very traumatic event. I still shudder at the thought of some of it and I was only marginally affected."

"That's what the therapist said, it will take time."

"Well, if it's any consolation, the people who did what they did to you are no longer around. I met with a Colonel in the CIF who routed out the militia, they no longer exist."

"Oh, what is the CIF?"

"Security Forces."

"Martin, Pa would like to talk to you."

"OK, put him on."

"Hello, this is Johann."

"Hello sir, pleased to talk to you."

"I believe we owe you a debt of great magnitude, our daughter is very precious to us and by all accounts, it is only due to you that she is still with us."

"That's very good of you to say that but I think anyone would have done the same under the circumstances."

"Maybe, maybe not. If ever you come to South Africa, you will receive a warm welcome from us."

"Thank you. I'll bear that in mind. My main concern is that Jo, sorry Johanna, is getting better."

"Yes, she is getting better but slowly; some days good, some not so good. Today is a good day, the newspaper article, Ma remembering the letter and now this telephone call have made Johanna very happy.

Once again thank you.

I will now give the telephone back to my daughter."

"Martin,"

"Hi,"

"Pa is very happy, I don't know what you said to him but you have made him smile."

"I'm glad that everything is working out for you, I will call you at least twice a week and we can email more often if you like.

I'm sure that we could talk all night but I think it would be wise not to tax you too much at one time. I would not want to be responsible for you having nightmares or flashbacks.

I'll see if I can cook up a plan to visit you in the near future, if that's OK?"

"Oh yes, that would be wonderful."

"OK, I'll be in touch, look after yourself and say cheerio to your parents for me. Bye."

Martin logged out of his email account and opened Google.

He typed in Willowmore, South Africa. Up came a map of the area, he enlarged it and scanned the nearby town names, ah ha, Steytlerville. The telephone area code was the same as Jo's. It looked like a small town east of Willowmore towards the coast, a good place to start.

He then typed in the search box. 'Nearest national airport to Steytlerville'. Port Elizabeth appeared.

British Airways was his next search. He took the number from the website and dialled it.

After a considerable wait, a cheerful lady answered.

"Good evening, British Airways, how may I be of assistance?"

"I'd like to book a flight to Port Elizabeth, South Africa please."

"Yes sir, you can do that on the website."

"Yes I know but I need to get there as soon as possible."

"I understand, if you can give me some details, I will make a booking. So, there are no direct flights to your destination, the flights that we can offer go via Johannesburg then an internal flight with a code share airline to Port Elizabeth. Would that be acceptable?"

"Yes, that's fine."

"If I may take some details?"

Martin gave the required information and paid with a credit card because the departure flight was booked for the following day an e-ticket was issued, which he printed off as soon as it appeared on his email.

Authorisation: BA 1236853
BA 0057 LHR-JNB Departing 21.25 Arriving 09.15 +1
BA 6241 JNB-PLZ Departing 11.10 Arriving 12.50
Return flight,
BA 6242 PLZ-JNB Departing 13.25 Arriving 15.00
BA 0056 JNB-LHR Departing 1920 Arriving 0530+1

A separate email was also printed off with the Avis hire car details.

Travel insurance sprang to mind, he had never needed it before. He had been covered under the company scheme.

Another search on Google and he was covered.

It was now late at night, he made his way to the bedroom and although he felt tired, he slept fitfully, eventually succumbing to full sleep according to his last look at the clock at around 03:35.

By 06:30, he was up and in the shower.

Breakfasted and ready to go, he packed his trusty rucksack, he would travel light, even though he had made his outward and inbound flights a month apart he didn't want to be encumbered with a suitcase, if he needed more clothes, he would buy them. He was taking plenty of cash. He didn't like using credit cards in Africa, too many crooks.

He organised a taxi to the train station for 16:00. That should give plenty of time before check-in but also a lot of time to kill between now and then.

He tidied his flat, it wasn't large but it took time, he drove his car into his garage, connected the battery charger and locked the doors.

The shopping that he had bought the day before he decided to give to the elderly couple who lived across the hallway. Knocking the door, he stood waiting with a carrier bag in each hand.

Glynis opened the door.

"Oh, going away again Martin, I thought you'd retired?"

"I have but I'm going to see a friend and take a holiday," he handed her the groceries, "not sure how long I'll be gone."

"Oh, don't worry we'll keep an eye on your flat for you. Have a nice holiday and thanks for these. What time are you leaving?"

"Got a taxi booked for 16:00, I have a couple of hours yet."

Those two hours seemed to last for ever but at last the taxi appeared in the car park. Martin grabbed his rucksack, had a last look around and left, locking the door securely.

At the bottom of the stairway were the residents' mailboxes. Out of habit, he checked his. Inside was a brown cardboard backed envelope with DO NOT BEND printed in red on the front face. It was addressed to him with a 'University of Winchester' franking mark.

Time to look at that later, he thought as he placed it into the front pocket of his rucksack.

"Lymington Station please." He instructed the driver as he made himself comfortable.

Sitting in Terminal 5 at Heathrow, his boarding pass in his pocket Martin realised that he hadn't booked a hotel.

A search on the internet found a small guest house just off the main street in Steytlerville, it had good reviews and was not too expensive.

He booked a room for three nights and paid for one night with his credit card, he would use cash for further charges when he got there.

The few extra inches in Premium Economy helped aid a good night's sleep, along I might add, with a couple of drinks.

Martin was awoken by the rattle of the breakfast trolley and the opening of the window blinds by those passengers wanting to see the sunrise.

It was just after six in the morning, three hours to go.

The immigration formalities at Johannesburg airport were fairly quick and not having baggage helped at customs, a change of terminals (A to B) and there was still time for a coffee before boarding the flight to Port Elizabeth.

Chapter 20

The staff at the Avis desk had everything ready to go. All they needed was a swipe of his credit card.

They provided a map just in case the on-board Sat Nav failed, the car was fuelled and had to be returned with a full tank.

"There is a petrol station at the airport." he was informed.

The road was apparently quite fast and of good quality, about 185 kilometres, should take about two hours.

After finding his way out of town and onto the M4, the road was as he had been told, the Sat Nav was giving clear instructions.

Barring any problems, he would be in Steytlerville before it became dark.

"Welcome to Steytlerville," the road sign announced. Martin slowed down as he drove into the main street, looking for the sign to the guest house.

The yellow painted building surrounded by a similarly coloured high wall with an electrically operated sliding gate, was set in a large well-tended colourful garden just off the main street, it was cool and welcoming inside.

Check-in formalities out of the way, Martin made his way to his room, he showered and headed for the bar, it was close to sunset and the heat of the sun was already abating.

With an ice-cold beer in his hand, he grabbed a local newspaper and a tourist pamphlet and sat in the garden to enjoy the serenity.

He decided that he would call Jo in the morning, that way he would be refreshed and able to take whatever was thrown at him, not that he expected any trouble.

Breakfasted and dressed in clean un-creased clothes, he called Jo's number, it was 09:00 and he was expecting her to be up.

"Hallo, de Klerk Plaas."*

"Hi, may I speak to Johanna please?"

"I am afraid that's not possible, she has gone out."

"Oh, when will she be back?"

"You must be Martin, with an accent like that."

"Yes, I am, I presume that you must be Johanna's mother?"

"Yes, Johanna has gone into town with her Pa, they will be back in maybe one and a half to two hours, you should call after that."

"I'll do that, can you please tell her that I called?"

"Of course."

"Thank you, bye."

Martin put down the receiver, feeling more than a little deflated.

'Oh well, I might just as well go for a walk,' he thought to himself.

'One of the tourist pamphlets mentioned a museum, good place to start,' he thought. When he got to it, he found that it was shut. Not my day.

Walking back to the hotel, he smelled fresh coffee, I could just do with a cup of that he thought and followed his nose.

The delicious aroma was coming from a small building on Sarel Cilliers Street and was appropriately called 'The Coffee Shop'.

He ordered a freshly ground cup of hot coffee and despite having eaten a large breakfast not more than two hours before, he also ordered a Danish pastry.

Walking back to the guest house, he saw a man and a woman loading a box into the back of a Ford pickup truck, he stopped, looked again at the woman, she still had her back to him but he was sure.

"Jo," he called out.

The woman stiffened and turned, wide-eyed. The older man beside also turned and looked towards Martin.

"Martin, Martin," the woman shouted and came running over to him. Tears of joy filling her eyes, hugging him so tightly that he couldn't breathe.

"Hi Jo," he gasped, "I thought I'd surprise you."

"Oh my goodness!" She turned to the man that she had been helping to load the box into the truck and said, "Pa, this is Martin, from England."

Martin offered his hand to Jo's father, who took it with a bone-crunching grasp.

"Pleased to meet you Martin," he said. At the same time, looking Martin over thoroughly, as though trying to see his inner soul.

Martin was acutely aware of being appraised.

"I guess your daughter failed to mention my age," he said.

"Age was never mentioned but regardless of that, we are very grateful to you for enabling the return of our daughter."

Jo was hanging onto Martin's arm.

"When did you get here, where are you staying? How did you know where to come?" She asked all in one breathe.

"OK, OK, I arrived last night, I came in through Port Elizabeth, I have a room at the Steytlerville guest house and if you remember, you told me only two days ago that you go to Willowmore hospital for therapy, I looked it up, checked telephone area codes and decided that Steyterville would be a good place to start my search. I called your home this morning and your mother told me that you had gone into town with your father and to call back later.

It was just luck that I was out for a walk because not only have I come to the right town I also found you in it."

"You came all this way to see me?"

"Well yes and also because your father said that he would buy me a beer." Winking at her father as he said it.

"You're joking, yes, about the beer."

"Of course I'm joking, English sense of humour I'm afraid.

I have come to see you and if necessary, help with your recovery."

"You must come to the farm, meet my Ma and stay with us, no need to stay in town."

"I think that will depend on your father, Pa I mean."

Jo looked at her Pa. he shrugged his shoulders and said,

"Maybe Mr Martin wishes to stay in town."

"I have booked a room for three nights, if you think that it would be acceptable for me to stay with yourselves, I would be most happy to accept, otherwise I will stay in town until I leave. I do not wish to impose. I realise that my arrival here is not due to your invitation, and please, call me Martin."

"I should discuss the matter with Anika, my wife, it is only right."

"Of course."

"But you should come to the house and meet her first."

"Oh yes, you can come with us now, there's room in the truck," Jo said.

"It might be better if I follow you, I have a car and that way I won't need to be brought back into town later."

"OK, I'll stay here with you, Pa can go home and I'll show you the way when you get your car."

133

Jo's Pa looked at her with concern on his face.

"Are you sure?" He asked her.

"Oh yes, I'm going to be OK. I know the way home."

"That isn't what your Pa means." I said.

"No, I know. It's OK Pa, I feel safe with Martin. We will be home soon."

Her Pa climbed into his truck and with an expression of concern still on his face, he drove away.

"Right, I think that we had better get the car, I don't want your father coming after me because you're late getting home."

Jo giggled.

A ten minute walk and they entered the guest house. Rosie, the owner was standing at the reception desk, she knew Jo.

"Hello Johanna, it's nice to see you out and about, you're obviously getting better," Looking around, she asked, "Are your parents outside?"

"No, Pa has gone home. This is Martin," she said, introducing me. "He is staying here."

"Yes, I know, I signed him in last evening. How do you know him?"

"Martin is the person who helped me in Mozambique, he is the man who saved my life." Then she started to cry.

"Oh my god!"

"Hey Jo don't cry, that's all over, you're safe now," Martin said putting his arms around her and holding her close.

"Remember you saved my life as well."

"I did? How?"

"After we had left the cave and come down the mountain, we camped overnight near some bushes, out in the grassland. We had just got ready to move on the next morning when you said to me firmly, 'Don't Move' then you slowly pulled the machete from my rucksack and whoosh, and you slashed at something behind me.

A Mamba you said, if I remember correctly."

"Oh Johanna," said Rosie, "how brave, those snakes are deadly."

"I don't remember," replied Jo but then as if a door had opened somewhere in her mind, she said, "didn't we get on a bus that day?"

"We did. Armed to the teeth and you managed to find somewhere to sit whereas I had to stand."

Addressing Rosie, Martin said. "I am just going to collect my car keys and drive Jo home."

Jo went with Martin to his room, they sat for a while admiring the view of the garden. Eventually, Martin grabbed the keys from the safe where he had placed his valuables and said,

"Right come on, let's go and meet your Ma."

Chapter 21

Leaving the guest house car park, Jo directed Martin to turn to the left along main street until out of the town.

"It's only a twenty-minute drive." she said, and then directed him to carry on until the next left turn, it was a gravel road and it led directly to the farm.

"It all seems such a long time ago," Jo said, "What have you been doing since then? Are you still working in Mozambique?"

"It's a long story and I have given up working anywhere. I've retired.

After you were sent to South Africa, I returned to my base in Cuamba and then decided I just wanted to enjoy life, that brush with death and indeed the hard physical work of boring water holes had hardened my resolve to take things easy.

I left Mozambique and went home to the UK, intending never to return but after a few months, I got bored and remembering those wonderful cave paintings, I contacted a local university about them. I ended up back in Mozambique with two academics showing them what we had found. I was there for ten days before returning with them to the UK.

That reminds me, I have an envelope in my rucksack from the university. I found it in the post box as I left my flat."

The farmhouse came into view before Jo could pose a question.

"I have a question for you," Martin asked as he pulled up in front of the house.

He could hear dogs barking, sounded like from behind the house.

"Yes?"

"Should I call you Jo or Johanna?"

"Between us Jo is fine but my parents are quite old fashioned, so Johanna when with them would be best."

"OK, so how should I address your parents?"

"I will ask."

By the time they had exited the car, both of Jo's parents were waiting on the stoep for them.

Jo half-dragged Martin towards her parents,

"Ma, this is Martin. He's come all this way to find me!"

Martin offered his hand to Jo's mother but instead of taking it, she walked forward and clasped him in her arms.

"I want to thank you for saving our daughter," she said, "she is our only child and she is very precious to us. Thank-you is such a small word but I do not know what else to say."

"There is no need to say anything, I did what I thought was the right thing to do, I would like to think that others would also have done the same."

"Pa, Ma, Martin wants to know how he should address you?"

"Johann is good with me," her Pa answered.

"Then Anika will also be alright for me," said her Ma. "Come let us go inside, I have prepared some refreshments."

The farmhouse was made of rendered blockwork and painted cream. The roof appeared to be of corrugated metal with a deep overhang all around the house.

It was cool inside and despite the overhanging roof, surprisingly light.

Martin was offered a comfortable armchair in which to sit, Jo's Pa sat in one of the same while Jo and her Ma sat on a large leather sofa.

The seating arrangement was separated by a low wooden table upon which stood a pot of coffee, a bowl of sugar and a small jug of milk, cups and saucers. A plate of home-made cookies was also there.

"Please help yourself Martin," Anika said.

"Thank you."

Looking at Jo's parents, he said.

"You must have many questions to ask regarding not just about me but also of what your daughter had experienced over those days before she was transferred home.

I have come here not just to see and potentially help Johanna but also to perhaps help you understand the trauma that she went through."

"That period of time was the most traumatic experience that I have ever gone through and whilst it was not all bad, a lot of it was."

"Jo, sorry Johanna has told me that she has not regained her memory fully yet, maybe that is a good thing but I can perhaps tell you what happened, sparing your daughter further stress."

Johann looked directly at Martin,

"Thank you, we will talk at some length I think about this but for now I have work to do, I have sheep to feed and water. The land here as you will have noticed, is not the most hospitable and the animals need a little assistance to survive."

After Johann had left and the coffee and cookies were finished, Anika cleared the table asking Jo to help her in the kitchen.

Martin stood on the stoep surveying the land around the farmhouse.

"Ma likes you," said a voice behind him.

He turned to see Jo grinning from ear to ear.

"Oh, thank goodness for that, I'd hate to be on the most wanted list!"

She looked at him, obviously not quite comprehending what he meant.

"Most wanted list?"

"Yes, you know, like the baddies in the movies, everybody chasing after them."

"Oh yes, I see what you mean."

"Come, I'll show you around."

The farmstead was fairly compact, just a few outbuildings to store equipment and foodstuff and a much larger covered holding area for the sheep that would be sent to the market.

"Most of our farm is in the bush," Jo explained, "Pa is always out mending fences trying to keep not only the sheep in but also the predators out."

"I guess the dogs that I heard barking are sheep dogs then?"

"Not really, guard dogs would be a more appropriate term, they're 'Ridgebacks', very strong and dependable."

"I hope you feed them well, I don't fancy losing an arm!"

"Oh no, we keep them a little hungry, it keeps them ready for action."

They went back into the coolness of the farmhouse where Anika was busy preparing the evening meal.

"I hope you will stay for dinner Martin? I don't think the guest house serves evening meals and the hotel restaurant may be fully booked."

"Yes, thank you, I will, it smells delicious."

"Nothing fancy, lamb of course with herbs and spices."

Jo gave Martin a tour of the farmhouse and then they settled in the chairs out on the stoep.

"I knew that it must have been you that disclosed the details of the cave as soon as I read it in the newspaper."

"Sorry, I don't understand."

"You told me earlier that you took two academics to the cave."

"Yes, that's correct. But I don't know anything about a newspaper. We left Mozambique without telling anyone, well except my ex-boss, who had organised our transport. Nick and Lisa, the academics told me that they would let me know when the Dig was finished, maybe that's what is in the envelope that I have in my rucksack."

"Pa showed me an article in the Herald, it said that the Mozambique ministry of culture had discovered a cave with spectacular paintings and was protected by a wonder of nature if I remember correctly, it also said something about English universities helping. I will find the newspaper."

She disappeared into her bedroom and came out a few minutes later, brandishing a news page.

Handing it to Martin, she said,

"Here, you can read it yourself while I get us a coffee."

Martin read the article and waited for Jo to return.

"It's obvious what has happened," he said as Jo sat down beside him.

"The universities would have had to inform the Mozambique authorities of the discovery, we discussed this before we returned to the UK. They would then have had to apply to those authorities for permission to carry out the 'Dig' as they called it. I guess Mozambique couldn't wait to tell the world."

"Dr Nick Trulade is head of Archaeology at Winchester University and Professor Lisa McLaren is a geologist specialising in Tectonics at Southampton University.

It will be interesting to read what they have sent me although that might have to wait a while as I think that the envelope contains a CD and I didn't bring my computer."

"That's not a problem, I have mine. We can read it on that."

"Well, it will still have to wait until tomorrow. It's in my rucksack at the guest house."

"You must still have a lot to tell me though?"

"Probably but why don't you tell me what you have been doing, the last time I saw you, you were lying on a hospital bed, heavily sedated and then you were shipped out before I could say good-bye."

"There are a lot of periods that I cannot remember, I woke up or at least was woken up in hospital in Pretoria. I had been there for several weeks, my wounds," she shuddered at the thought, "had healed but my mental state was probably fragile and is still uncertain. I have a therapy session once a month, it seems to help.

I suffer from bad dreams, nightmares actually but thankfully not too often and as I have said, periods of memory loss, like the episode with the mamba that you mentioned earlier."

"But," Martin interjected, "my reminding you of that seemed to jog some memories back, you remembered the bus."

"Yes, the psychiatrists have told me that trigger words or even similar events may unlock memories both good and bad."

"I will need to be careful what I say then."

"Johanna," her Ma called from the kitchen, "Pa will be back soon, I need some help with the food."

Johann came into the house, back from tending his sheep.

"Come," he said to Martin. "I will give you the beer that you came for." smiling as he said it.

They sat on the stoep, the glasses of cold beer, condensing in the late afternoon heat.

After a few mouthfuls of the cold liquid, Johann turned to Martin and said,

"Let us talk. Please tell me everything you can about what happened to Johanna."

"I'll start at the beginning."

Martin described the arrival of the militia into the village, the noise, the shooting and what he heard happening in the hut.

Johann's face went red, then purple with rage as Martin described the events and the condition that he found Johanna to be in when he rescued her.

"As ek ooit daardie bastards kry," he stopped, "sorry, I say in English. If I ever find those bastards, I'll tear them apart with my bare hands."

"There's no need, they have been dealt with in a manner that fits their crimes."

"What do you mean, how do you know this?"

"I gave information of their whereabouts to a Colonel in the security forces, he dealt with them, all of them and I have seen the result of his action.

It was not a pretty sight but they got what they deserved. They will not hurt anyone else."

Martin was still talking when Jo called them in for dinner.

"We can continue this later?" Johann asked.

"Of course, it will be best perhaps if Johanna is not within listening distance."

The meal was superb, fresh 'Karoo' lamb in a rich spicy sauce with locally grown vegetables, complimented with a few glasses of South African Merlot and a large helping of 'Malva' pudding and custard.

"Wow! That was superb," Martin told Anika, "I don't think I could manage another morsel, no matter how tempting it may be."

While Jo and her Ma cleared and washed the dishes, Martin told Johann a little more.

Johann smiled when Martin answered his question about what going 'commando' meant and his use of the wound dressings but was otherwise silent as Martin continued to narrate the events.

He had just gotten to the arrival at the cave when the tinkle of coffee cups signalled the end of the conversation.

Johanna, bearing a cup in each hand came out onto the stoep, the delicious aroma preceding her by a few seconds; her Ma followed shortly after also holding two cups of hot coffee.

"We thought that you men had talked enough and would probably be in need of this," said Anika.

They drank their coffee out in the open, listening to the crickets and other nocturnal creatures while gazing out the wide expanse of star encrusted sky, the like of which you can only see in the wide open light pollution free space of Africa.

"I think it is time for me to head back to the guest house, I do not wish to outstay my welcome and I do not want to encounter some wild beast on my way either.

If it is OK with you all, I would like to return tomorrow, I will bring the CD that the university have sent me and perhaps you might like to view what is on it."

"Oh Martin, do you have to go so early?"

"It's not that early and I'm sure your parents have things to talk about.

I'll see you tomorrow and maybe we can open a few more doors of your memory."

"Yes child," her Ma said, "I think that we have all done enough for today."

It took a little longer driving back in the dark, partly because everything looked different but also because Martin was being cautious about loose animals.

After parking the car, he sat in the garden outside of his room, taking in the beauty of the surroundings, breathing in the aroma of the flowers and once more marvelling at the myriad of twinkling stars of the Milky Way high above.

Chapter 22

As he drove into the farm courtyard the next morning Jo appeared on the stoep.

"Come on lazy bones," she called, "Pa's been waiting for you."

He was ushered through the house, past Ma and out of the back door. Johann was sitting on a quad bike, two large dogs standing beside it.

"Walk over slowly, the dogs won't hurt you unless you run. This is Max," he pointed to the larger dog, "and that one is Samson, they are my protectors when I am in the bush. Come, you are quite safe, let them smell you."

Martin did as he was told.

"There, now you are friends."

"Have you ridden a quad before?"

"No but I did have a motorcycle."

"OK, a little different to handle but similar in many ways. Johanna, give Martin the helmet."

"I thought you might like to see some more of the farm."

"That would be good," Martin replied, but secretly thinking that Johann just wanted to get him on his own.

They set off, Max and Samson running effortlessly alongside Johann's quad as they bumped along over rocks and mounds of baked earth.

Stopping at a high point, Johann switched off his machine, Martin did the same.

"You see that 'Koppie' [11] over there, that's the Northern boundary of the farm and the rise to the East is the boundary there, the river forms another and the highway the last. Quite big enough for a small farmer like me."

"It's very impressive, and quite beautiful. How many sheep do you have?"

"At the moment, only one hundred and forty, come the lambing season we will more than double that figure."

---

[11] Rocky outcrop

They stood in silence for a moment, the dogs alert, sniffing the air for some unseen predator.

"I get the impression that we are here for more than a look at your land, Johann. If you have questions, fire away."

"You are very perceptive. I would like you to continue from where you stopped last evening, here there are no other ears."

Martin took up the story from when they found the cave, he described how when trying to collect the moss he found the entrance, the discovery of the paintings, of the demise of the three militiamen and the bounty they left behind; continuing on, he described their leaving the cave, trekking across the bush and Jo's bravery with the snake.

"Very venomous, the Mamba," Johann said.

His description of the boarding of the bus, armed to the teeth elicited another laugh from Johann.

"Come," he said, "if we don't go back now I think they might send out a search party."

Max and Samson bounded on ahead, stopping every so often and looking back as though to check the master was still with them.

Coffee and sandwiches were waiting for them on the kitchen table when they walked through the door.

"I thought you'd gotten lost," said Jo. "I wanted to come looking for you but Ma said the smell of coffee would bring you back."

"Aren't mothers always right!"

"Well in this case, yes."

"Just a minute, I have to get something from the car."

Walking back into the house, he handed Jo a CD.

"This is what Nick sent me. According to the note enclosed with it, it is a draft copy of the teams-findings at the cave. If you can boot up your computer, it may answer a few questions, perhaps help your memory."

Enter Password!

"Ah, err, wait a minute, there is something on the note, yes, flight number home required!"

"Try BA0056."

BA0056.

The disc whirled and up came the Winchester University Logo.

Draft was printed across the heading.

Initial Report of the findings of a Joint expedition by the Ministry of Culture and Tourism and the Archaeological and Geological Departments of the universities of Winchester and Southampton United Kingdom.

"Oh my goodness!"

"Looks like a lot to read, wait, photographs. Scroll through to them."

Jo scrolled down the contents list and clicked the mouse button on the photographs heading.

There in front of them was a picture of the magnificent Ox like creature, the same one that Jo and Martin had seen in the cave but here on the screen it looked even better.

Everyone was in awe.

They spent the next thirty minutes gazing at the wonderful, brightly coloured images on the screen, images of the pool were also included and taken from above presumably with the aid of a camera-equipped drone they could see the vortex in the water.

The last images looked out of focus or fogged over and hard to view, Martin straining hard suddenly realised what they were looking at.

"Those photos have been taken in the pool, they must have had an underwater camera on a remote-control cable, look here," he pointed to several large objects, "those look like rocks and that, good grief, that looks like a rifle! I dropped one in the pool before we left."

"Because we had three and there were only two of us," Jo said and her hand flew to her mouth in an attempt to stifle a laugh, it failed. She sat there in front of the computer, spluttering over the screen, tears rolling down her bright red cheeks, trying to control a fit of infectious laughter.

"What is the matter child?" her concerned Ma asked.

"Nothing," she replied, "absolutely nothing is wrong. An image appeared in my head of Martin, naked by the pool with rifles across his back, struggling to put his rucksack on the wrong way round. I don't know where it came from, it just popped into my head."

They all looked at Martin.

"Well, that's because it happened. I went to collect the belongings of the three militiamen who had jumped into the pool and I was naked because it took such a long time to dry clothes in the cave. You laughed at me then too and, I might add, made other comments. Presumably, the photo jogged your memory."

"Naked!" Anika exclaimed.

"Completely."

"Johanna has seen naked men before, after all she is a nurse and I can see the logic. No sense standing around in wet clothes," said Johann.

"What other comments?"

"Oh, something about an 'Almost white body bobbing about'."

Jo blushed and turned her attention to the computer screen.

"There is such a lot of information on this disc it will take hours to read."

"Well don't worry, you can keep it for when you've got nothing better to do."

"Johanna, come and help me set the table for lunch, your father has work to do after."

"Martin, you will come with me, yes." It was a command rather than a question.

"Sure, I'll be happy too." sensing that Johann was anxious to hear the rest of the story.

They bumped along the rough tracks to the far side of farm's land, Max and Samson happily trotting alongside, as before their ears and eyes alert for any signs of predators.

"This dry weather is causing a lot of hardship, the land is not ideal for sheep but we can manage if the rains come when they should, until then I must feed and water them. Many of the farmers around here are selling up and moving out."

The sheep came running over as the food was tipped into the troughs, jostling each other out of the way, eager to fill their bellies.

Johann turned his attention to the water trough.

"Come," he said, "I need to clean this trough, you can pump the water while I scrub. Now, you can continue with your account. You had just boarded a bus if I recollect."

Martin continued as requested, he told of the kindness and excellent medical help of Dr Fernandes, of the arrival of the 4x4 from UMA and of his suspicions of the driver and his assistant, and placing his pistol in his waist band as a precaution.

His description of the death of Dr Tom and of Jo's reaction caused Johann's face to contort with rage, he only relaxed when Martin explained how he, in turn, shot the murderer and forced the driver to stop the vehicle.

Johann's rage once again surfaced as Martin told of the driver's action in holding a pistol to Jo's head before turning to shoot Martin.

Ending the story with Jo's removal to South Africa, he could see that the story had had an effect on Johann far greater than he might have guessed.

"We owe you a great deal, far more than a simple thank you can convey but believe me, we are very glad that you were there and willing and able to help."

He was silent for a minute and then said,

"You told me that the militia have been dealt with. How do you know this?"

"I showed Colonel Almeida where I thought the militia were hiding, he had brought some aerial photos of the area. I indicated the location from them. A few days later, it was announced on TV that the militia had been located and wiped out in a fire fight with the security forces, not only that but the Colonel telephoned to say that it had been done."

"Hmm but politicians are not known for being truthful!"

"I agree but I have seen the result for myself."

"How?"

"I passed by the camp with Nick and Lisa, the university guys, on our way back to civilisation. I can tell you there was nothing left but a few burnt huts and vehicles and a stinking, rotting pile of half-burnt decomposing corpses. The Colonel had done his job, for sure. Espada de Cristo is no more."

On entering the farmhouse, Jo came over to Martin and said,

"Rosie Botha called, she wanted to know if you were needing the room for a bit longer, apparently you only booked for three nights. Ma told me to tell her to book you in for at least another week, is that OK?"

"Oh gosh, I completely forgot about that, yes, at least a week. My visa is valid for three months and I will stay as long as it takes or at least until I outstay my welcome."

Jo smiled from ear to ear.

Chapter 23

When Martin entered the reception area of the guest house that evening, Rosie was sitting behind the counter concentrating on a pile of paperwork and she looked up.

"Sorry Rosie, I should have requested a longer stay this morning. How much do I owe you?"

"There is nothing to pay."

"Beg your pardon!"

"Menheer de Klerk [12] has already paid. You are booked in for seven more days and if you wish to extend the time, please let me know as soon as possible."

"Yes, of course."

The following morning, Martin was up early and drove out to the farm house with a bag of dirty clothes on the backseat.

Rosie had told him that the nearest laundromat was in Willowmore. He also wanted to buy some more clothes and the shops he needed for them were there also.

After accepting a cup of strong coffee and thanking Johann for paying his hotel bill, he asked if it would be OK for Johanna to accompany him to Willowmore.

"I realise that she has not been away from either of you for a while and if you think it will be too traumatic, I understand."

"Why do you want to go to Willowmore?"

"I have some laundry that needs doing and I need to buy some more clothes. I only brought enough for a few days."

"Johanna has to go to there tomorrow, she has an appointment with Dr Dhal. You can come with us if you like? We usually shop after her appointment. If you give me your washing, I will put it in the machine now."

---

[12] Mr de Klerk

"Thank you, if it will be no trouble."

"Of course not."

"Johann! This Dr Dhal, is he a psychiatrist?"

"He is a she, Dr Sangita Dhal and yes she is. Why?"

"I wonder if perhaps I should talk to her, tell her the events that happened to Johanna, it might help with the diagnosis and treatment?"

"A good idea. You can suggest it tomorrow if you go with them."

"OK, but how about if I could speak to the doctor today, give some advance info before tomorrow's appointment."

"Good thinking. Anika, can you call Dr Dhal and let Martin speak to her."

"Here Martin, Dr Dhal."

"Good morning, Mr Martin."

"Actually, it's Newman, Martin Newman. But Martin is fine."

"I'm sorry."

"No need to be."

"I understand that you may have some information that might help in the treatment of Miss de Klerk. Am I correct in thinking you are the Martin that she alludes to in her description of events?"

"You are correct. I have come to South Africa in order to help her and if that means talking to her doctor, then I will be happy to do so. I understand that Johanna has an appointment with you tomorrow, I can come along with her then or if it will help, I could come and brief you today."

"I have a busy schedule as you might guess but if you can be here for 12:30, my lunch break, we can talk then."

"Yes, I can do that, I believe it takes about two hours to get Willowmore so if I leave fairly soon, I should be with you by then."

Dr Dhal ate her lunch in her office. She was brushing the remains of a samosa from her blouse when Martin was shown in.

She was immaculately dressed in a brightly coloured two-piece suit with a sparkly white blouse that showed off her slim figure.

She was not a typical looking 'shrink'.

Her handshake was firm and warm,

"Please sit down, Mr Newman."

"Martin please."

"Yes, sorry you did tell me earlier. How do you think you can help Miss de Klerk? Please be aware that I will be recording our conversation, it's nothing sinister, just for reference later."

"That's fine and if it's OK with you, I'll refer to her as Jo, I have done so since we first met and she is quite happy with it. I am aware of the trauma that she has suffered, I was with her for a lot of it and I am acutely aware that she has either lost or at least buried a lot of those memories. My aim in coming to see you is to give you the full picture of what she went through in order that you may perhaps be able to tailor her treatment to ensure a speedy and more complete outcome. I realise that her treatment may take a long time and so anything I can do to help must surely be advantageous."

"I commend and understand your reasoning, however, it remains to be seen as to whether anything that you tell me will be of help regarding her treatment."

"That's fine, I accept that you're the doctor and as they say, 'The doctor knows best'."

She nodded.

"Please start from the very first time you saw Jo."

Martin narrated in complete honesty and detail, leaving nothing out but adding nothing either, the doctor scribbling copious notes as he did so, only occasionally asking for clarification, her face showing no emotion.

A knock on the door brought a halt to the proceedings.

"Yes,"

The receptionist poked her head around the door.

"Your 1:45 appointment is here, Doctor."

"Thank you Judith, I'll see them shortly. Martin, we will have to continue this at a later time, it is most useful information and I need to hear the complete story before I can adjust Jo's treatment to ensure that it is most beneficial. I will arrange some time to talk to you again shortly, my diary is quite full, so I will have to reschedule some appointments. How will I be able to contact you?"

"Just leave a message with Jo's parents."

Martin felt as if a weight had been lifted from his shoulders, talking to Dr Dhal although for Jo's sake had helped to ease his turmoil, here was someone who could use the information to its best advantage.

Jo was waiting on the stoep when he drove back into the farmyard, it was only when he got out of the car that he realised that he forgotten to go shopping.

'Oh well, I'll have to go back tomorrow,' he thought.

"Well, what did she say? Will I be cured?"

"Eventually but it may take a while." He smiled. "Actually, we didn't discuss you at all, doctor/client privilege I guess, you can ask her tomorrow."

Martin sat in the back of Anika's car, the journey although the same as the one that he had taken yesterday seemed shorter, maybe it was because he was not alone.

Jo was shown into the doctor's office and Martin and Anika sat in comfortable chairs in the anti-room.

"Martin, will you answer me a question?"

"If I can."

"It's personal, for Johanna but important."

"OK."

"Johann has told me everything you told him, I know Johanna was raped."

"Yes, brutally so."

"But she is not pregnant!"

"Thankfully."

"How is this possible?"

Martin sensed that he was being backed into a corner.

"I asked the same question to Dr Fernandes, he told me that nature sometimes lends a helping hand. He also told me that he was aware that drugs were available to, shall we say, take care of matters, but being a Catholic Hospital, they did not hold such drugs. So, maybe nature did help."

"Maybe but results from a blood test taken in Pretoria Hospital showed traces of," she consulted a piece of paper that she had removed from her handbag, "Mifepristone and Misoprostol in the sample."

"What are they? Can't say I've ever heard of them."

"They cause an abortion."

"Oh, I don't know how she could have taken them, she was heavily sedated in both hospitals, she certainly couldn't self-administer even if she got hold of those pills."

"Maybe the blood sample was contaminated."

"I don't think so."

"Johann is unaware of this. I should like to keep it so."

"Of course, Johanna's health and well-being are all that matters and I will do all I can to ensure that is the case."

Dr Dhal's office door opened and Jo appeared.

"She won't tell me anything of what you told her but she wants to see you now." said Jo indignantly.

"Hello Martin. Johanna, I heard that. I've rescheduled my diary; can you make it for 16:00 on Thursday? It's the only time I can manage this week and next week is not much better."

"Sure, 16:00 Thursday it is. Come on ladies, coffee is on me. Then we can go shopping."

Thursday came along soon enough and at 15:45, Martin was sitting in the anti-room waiting to see Dr Dhal. Her assistant, Judith, sitting behind the reception desk was occupied with a mountain of paperwork.

An elderly lady came out of the office, supported by an equally elderly man.

"Thank you doctor, we'll see you in two weeks." the man said.

"Judith, if Mr Newman is out there, please send him in."

Martin entered the doctor's office. Dr Dhal was once again immaculately dressed but this time in a cerise coloured skirt and complimentary embroidered blouse.

He sat in the same chair as on his previous visit.

"Hello Martin. Thanks for coming. If you can continue from where you finished on your last visit I would be much obliged, if it helps I can play the last part on the tape."

"No need, I can remember where I left off. Shall I begin?"

Dr Dhal switched on the recording machine.

As before, leaving nothing out nor adding anything, he continued the story until the point that Jo had been shipped off to South Africa.

"Or at least that's where Greenlove had said she was going."

"I sense you have an issue with Mr Greenlove?"

"I do, I understand the medical privacy aspect but it was also the way he said it and the fact it was done in an underhand manner. I didn't even get time to say goodbye and wish her well."

"You obviously care deeply for Jo but are those feelings sexual or of a more romantic nature?"

"Neither, I am no cradle snatcher! When I found Jo in that hut, I made a vow to myself to get her to safety; yes, she is a very attractive young lady and if I was a good few years younger, I might have made a play for her. But I met Jo due to tragic and traumatic circumstances and my only wish is for her to recover fully and live a healthy and fulfilling life. I have never entertained sexual thoughts about her in any way. I am old enough to be her father, for goodness sakes.

I am a person who likes to complete what I set out to do, to honour a promise if you like, even to myself. I thought that when I delivered Jo to Uni-Med, my mission would be completed but then they whisked her away, leaving me with unanswered questions, which to be honest disturbed me.

As I have told you, I wrote a letter to Jo which remained unanswered for a long time and that I suppose fed my anxiety. I tried to put it aside but being the person that I am and being in a retirement mode, it ate away at me.

So, when I eventually received her email, I was overjoyed and I guess the implied invitation from her father to visit them was too good to turn down."

"Martin? May I ask you some personal questions?"

"If it will help Jo, yes."

"It will help me in my treatment regime for Jo."

"OK, fire away."

"Have you ever been married?"

"Yes, I divorced, eight years ago."

"May I ask the reason for divorce?"

"Saskia and I married late in life, we were both career-minded. We tried for a family but to no avail. It turns out I fire blanks."

Doctor Dhal raised an enquiring eyebrow and was about to speak but Martin continued.

"We were offered treatment but with no guarantee of success. Although Saskia was five years younger than me, her biological clock was ticking and if she was to have a child safely, then time was of the essence. We decided, after much soul-searching, to go our separate ways. The divorce was an amicable but heart wrenching decision."

"How long were you married?"

"Six and a half years."

"Are you in a relationship now?"

"Not really, I'm a normal heterosexual bloke, I enjoy the fruits of life as so to speak but without becoming attached. Look Doc, I came here today to help Jo, not to be analysed."

"Point taken, my professional interest sometimes gallops away."

"Doctor, may I ask you a question?"

"Of course."

153

"I received a computer disc just before I left the UK. It featured an expedition to the cave that Jo and I stayed in. Jo played it on her computer, we were all with her at the time and the photos of the cave paintings jogged Jo's memory, opened doors, shall we say. Would my telling her of some of the nicer aspects of our journey together be of help, given that you obviously have your own treatment regime for her?"

"That is a difficult question to answer. You could try but if she doesn't respond immediately, don't be surprised, equally, she may encounter blacker memories associated with the one that you have mentioned and that in itself could cause concern."

"I see, a bit of a conundrum. However, if it's OK with you, I would like to try. I also wondered if perhaps Jo and I could visit places outside of her immediate area, gently get her used to the wider world again. Nothing too far from home, just not so familiar?"

"Once again, a difficult question. The brain is a very complex and complicated organ, we still only know a fraction of how it works but what we do know is that what works for one person, may not work for another. You can try, perhaps increasing the distance or time away from familiar surroundings little by little. Just be prepared to make a hasty return."

"I will. Thank you."

"Thank you Martin and good luck. You can always call me if you need advice. We both have Jo's recovery as a priority."

Chapter 24

"Well? Are you going to tell me what she said?"

"Oh Jo, it wasn't a question and answer session, I just told her of our little adventure, filled in the gaps of your memory so she can amend your treatment to get you fully back to health and stop your nightmares.

What she did say, however, at my request, was that we could go on trips out of town, not far away but away from familiar places and faces to help you regain your independence. How does that sound?"

"We'd come home every day?"

"Of course and you would have your phone, so you could call and see your parents if you needed to."

"OK, I'll try but I will ask Ma and Pa first."

"Sure, why don't we go and see them now?"

"Why not? That seems like a good idea. You could start at the Elephant Park, it's not far away but could keep you occupied for more than a few hours and then there's always Willowmore, easy driving distances." said Pa.

"Sounds good to me," replied Martin. "But I'll let Johanna decide."

"Martin. Johanna's Ma and I have come to a decision, it concerns you."

"Oh?"

"We have decided that given what you have done and are doing for Johanna, it is not right that you should have to stay in the guest house. If you are willing, we would be very happy for you to stay here with us. We have room and given your plans, it might make it easier for you to go out sightseeing or whatever you decide to do."

"Thank you. I would be happy to accept but only if Johanna is happy with the arrangement."

"Of course I am, it's a great idea," She gave her parents a hug, a smile on her face.

The next few days were spent 'sightseeing' acting like regular tourists. Up at dawn each day, driving longer and further as long as Jo felt comfortable.

Although, when a large group of dark-skinned people came towards them while walking along the seafront in Port Elizabeth, Jo clung to Martin's arm with such ferocity that he was bruised.

But not once did she feel the need to call her parents.

After two days of not leaving the farm, Martin broached a question to Jo's Ma.

"Johanna seems to be much less on edge than when I first arrived, she is more 'alive' in herself. Don't you think?"

"Yes, I think you are correct."

"I was wondering if it would be OK with you for me to suggest a trip a bit further away, to Cape Town perhaps? It would of course mean staying away for a few days."

Anika looked at him.

"That's quite a distance, about 650 kilometres, you couldn't get back in a hurry. I will need to talk with Johann."

"Sure, it's just a thought. I won't mention to Johanna unless you are both happy with the idea. You could always come along if you wish."

"We have discussed your proposal and provided Johanna is happy with the idea and that she calls us regularly, we have no objections. We will need to know where you will be staying in case of an emergency, the mobile phone system does not always work."

"Of course. I will ask Johanna when we are all together, that way you will be able to see her reaction and gauge for yourselves whether or not she truly wants to go or is just being polite. I do not want her to feel under any obligation."

"Cape Town! I haven't been there for years." Exclaimed Jo, wiping away gravy from her chin, "But that's a long way, we couldn't come back that day."

"No, I was thinking of going for four or five days. It will take about six, six and a half hours driving each way and we would need a few days to see the sights. What do you think? Please don't think I will be upset if you say no, it will be a big step for you to take and I accept that only you can make that decision."

Jo looked at her parents, willing them to help her make a decision.

Johann said, "Martin is right, only you can make that decision, whatever you decide we will accept and support."

"It's a long way to go, can I think about it and tell you later Martin?"

"Of course you can, take as long as you like."

Chapter 25

They left early, the sun was just showing its golden rays over the rocky terrain. They were driving west chasing the darkness.

"I've booked two rooms at the Mount Nelson but if you don't like it, we can find somewhere else."

Seven and a half hours later, they pulled into the courtyard of the Mount Nelson Hotel, arguably Cape Town's most prestigious hotel. Set in the garden district and with awe inspiring views of Table Mountain, it was 'the' place to stay.

Check in was swift, two adjacent rooms, with a connecting door. If the receptionist was curious, she didn't show it. Martin, being a foreigner, had more forms to fill in than Jo.

A bellboy showed them to their rooms. Martin made sure that Jo was safe and happy in her room before entering his. He tipped the bellboy and shut and locked the door after he left.

Opening his half of the connecting door, he knocked on Jo's; she opened it instantly.

"Have you seen the view?" She asked.

"Give me time, I thought I'd best check on you first."

She pulled him to her open window. "Look, it's so beautiful and the smell of the flowers, absolutely heavenly."

It was late afternoon; the sky was that azure colour that only Africa has and the west side and top of the mountain were bathed in the golden glow of the sun.

"Right, a quick shower and then downstairs for something to quench our thirst before we make any decisions about what to do tonight."

"Actually, you had better call your parents first."

They sat on the terrace enjoying the contents of a bottle of chilled crisp cape Chardonnay.

"Let's not go out tonight. It's been a long day. I'd like to just sit here and relax, smell the flowers and watch the sun go down."

"Suits me. That was a long drive. We can order food to be served out here if you like."

The sun was streaming through the window, wispy white clouds adorned the sky as Martin; towel wrapped around his waist, his hair still dripping, opened the connecting door in answer to the loud rapping.

Jo was dressed and ready for the day ahead.

"Come on lazy bones, it's time for breakfast and I'm starving."

"Shall I go down like this or would you prefer that I dress first?"

"Don't be silly, just get a move on otherwise all the food will have been eaten and it will be too hot to go out."

Full from breakfast and ready to go, they caught a Red Route sightseeing bus from right outside the hotel. It took a circuitous route to the cable car station passing through the (old) district six, the financial centre and the Castle of Good Hope before arriving at the lower cable car station.

The car was fairly full and Jo was a little apprehensive about being so confined but she rallied gamely and by getting in last, she was by the door ready to be first out.

What a view!

Reaching the top, the view was even more spectacular, the Indian Ocean to the east as far as the eye could see and Cape Town, Table Bay and Robben Island in the other.

"Come on, we can see even more if we climb up to the beacon," said Jo.

It was getting hot, there was very little wind; time to catch the cable car back down, it was just as crowded but Jo was more relaxed about it.

They hailed a taxi,

"Victoria and Alfred Waterfront please," Martin told the driver.

It took twenty minutes and the driver dropped them by the Victoria Wharf Centre.

"Lunch first?" Martin asked.

"Oh yes, then I'll be ready to shop."

"I was afraid you'd say that, I thought we were sightseeing?"

"We are but a girl's got to shop, nothing like this in Steytlerville."

"OK, just don't buy too much unless you are going carry at least some of it."

"That food was so good, let's walk a while."

"Sure, why not. But it didn't taste as good as the Guinea fowl and mealy pap."

Jo looked at him quizzically for a few seconds, then her eyes lit with recognition.

"From the militiamen who came to the pool." She said, smiling.

They walked and talked and found themselves in the craft work shop area, dozens of shops selling mainly locally made products with international brands thrown in for good measure.

It was packed with tourists and locals alike. A throbbing mass of humanity.

Jo was hanging on to Martin as though her life depended on it.

"OK let's get away from here," he said, as he did so Jo's grip became even stronger, when he looked, she was hyperventilating and staring to the left.

A group of black youths were coming through the crowd in their direction, not for any reason in particular, just heading towards them.

Martin looked around, spied a shop immediately to his right and half-dragged Jo through the door.

"Oh my goodness, is she alright?" The woman standing behind the counter asked as they burst through the doorway.

"She will be in a minute, I hope. Just a little frightened."

"Precious, come quickly, bring a chair."

A slim black woman with deep scars to her face and forearms came through a curtain, carrying a small rattan chair.

"Please sit, madam," she said to Jo.

"What has happened?" The shopkeeper asked Martin.

"Jo was attacked a while ago. I guess the crowds out there have been a little too much."

"Cape Town can be a bad place, you and your daughter can stay here as long as you like."

"Thank you but Jo is not my daughter and she wasn't attacked in Cape Town."

"Oh, I'm sorry."

"No need to be sorry, it's a reasonable assumption to make."

"Can you tell me what happened?"

Looking at Jo for approval before he answered, she nodded tacitly, he said.

"Jo was attacked whilst working with a medical team at a tribal village in Mozambique. I managed to get her away and eventually to safety. This trip to Cape Town is part of her, I guess you could say, rehabilitation. Maybe it was too soon."

"The poor girl,"

Turning to Jo, she said, "Jo you're safe here, you're in good hands and you can stay as long as you need. When you want to go, I can arrange a taxi if that's what you want. Precious will get you anything you need."

"Perhaps it might be better if you go into the back room, it will be quieter and no one will see you."

The back room was actually the storeroom, full of racks of local artwork and handicraft.

Precious fussed around, making sure Jo could want for nothing, holding her hand and comforting her like a mother would a sick child.

"You go out there sir, I will look after lady."

"Oh, OK. Jo, I'll be the other side of the curtain if you need me."

People came and went, business was brisk but between customers, Margarette the shop owner, chatted non-stop.

She was originally from Holland and had moved to Cape Town twenty years ago, married then divorced a 'pig' of a man and eventually set up a shop to sell locally made handicrafts.

"The women here can have a rough time," she said, "and not just the black girls."

"Martin," Jo called from behind the curtain. "I feel better now. Can we go back to the hotel?"

The curtain was pulled aside and Jo was stood there, looking a little sheepish but otherwise OK.

Margarette organised a taxi and as they were leaving the store, she passed them both a business card.

"I've put my mobile number on the back, if you need any help just call me. I'm here every day until eight. Just show this card to the taxi driver and he will bring you here, out of hours call me and I'll give directions."

She gave Jo a hug and shook Martin's hand.

"Precious will take you to the taxi."

As Jo was about to get into the taxi, Precious ran forward and hugged Jo tightly, saying in a quiet voice,

"Ons wat oorleef help mekaar," before returning to the shop.

Sitting in the taxi enroute to the hotel, Martin asked,

"What did Precious say to you, it sounded like Afrikaans?"

"It was," she said, "We survivors help each other. Did you see her scars?"

"Yes, I thought they were probably tribal markings."

"No, they were a present from a drunken ex-husband."

"Margarette runs a charity for women who have suffered domestic or other violence, all the goods they sell are made by the women that the charity helps."

Martin took the business card from his pocket.

"Cape Women's Refuge. Margarette Groen. Director."

They spent the rest of the day in the hotel, initially walking in the grounds, finally relaxing on the terrace until the last of the sun's rays disappeared and the inky blackness of the night sky was all around before enjoying a light meal in the restaurant.

Chapter 26

Martin was woken by the sound of muffled sobbing, they had left the adjoining doors open and the noises were coming from Jo's room.

It was still night-time and his room was lit by beams of moonlight streaming through the partly open shutter leaves, he slipped out of bed and padded across the thick carpet to the doorway. Jo was lying on her bed, her body convulsing in time with her sobs.

He sat beside her, gently brushing his hand across her cheek, re-assuring her that all was well, that she was just having a bad dream.

"Martin, I'm frightened, will you stay with me?" She asked.

"Of course, I'll stay as long as you want."

She pulled back the bed cover,

"Please, will you hold me, make me feel safe?"

He slid into the bed beside her and cradled her in his arms, it took a while but eventually her anguish subsided and she fell into a deep sleep.

Rays of sunlight piercing the shutters woke Martin, he was still cradling Jo in his arms, she had not moved all night. Carefully, he extracted himself from her bed and made for the shower in his room.

He was just about to shave when he heard her anxious call.

"Martin, where are you?"

With a bright red towel around his waist, he walked into his bedroom. Jo was standing by his bed.

She looked at him, then burst out laughing,

"Oh Martin, I thought you had gone," she said between bouts of laughter, "you look so funny, like 'Papa Noel' but not so fat."

It was then that he realised the reason for the laughter, the shaving foam.

"What did I say to you the last time you laughed at me?" he asked haughtily.

"I don't know, I really don't know!"

"I think I said, OK, I won't do it again." And he wiped the foam from his face using the towel from his waist.

This caused even more laughter from Jo because he was not wearing anything underneath, a small mistake on his part.

She ran to him and kissed him gently on the lips.

"I woke up and you were gone, your space was still warm so I knew that you had not been gone long but when I called, you didn't answer, I guess I was still a little frightened. I haven't had a dream like that for a while, it was so real."

"I guess it was to do with the episode in town yesterday, you were really frightened when that group of youths came our way. They weren't aggressive, just heading in the direction we had come from."

"You're probably right but I can't help it. Will I ever be normal again?"

"You are normal! You have suffered a huge trauma and it will no doubt take a long time for your brain to settle down. The Mind is like a maze with twisting passages, dead ends and secret doors. Every so often, you go down a passageway and find it blocked, that's when you can't remember something but then you go down another and a door opens, whether by an external trigger, like those youths yesterday or by your mind releasing information and of course what is behind that door may not always be pleasant.

Eventually, you will have been down all the passages and opened all the doors and that should end the bad dreams, at least that's my theory."

"You make it sound so simple."

"Like I said, that's my theory and I'm sticking to it, although Dr Dhal may disagree. Now! What would you like to do today?"

"I don't want to go anywhere crowded. I need to feel safe."

"Hmm, OK, how about a visit to a Vineyard? I've been looking through some pamphlets and there is a three hundred year old vineyard 'Vergelegen' it's called, not too far away. It's got good reviews, restaurants and even better, wine tasting. We could make a day of it."

"That sounds great. Do we just turn up or do we need to book?"

"I have the pamphlet, let me check. Oh, it says you must book, I'll give them a ring, you never know they might fit us in."

"Yes, OK, 11:30, no problem. Newman, great, thanks very much. Right, get your skates on, the tour starts at 11.30."

They arrived back at the hotel completely worn out, the tour of the vineyard was fantastic, driven around in a custom-built vehicle, shaded from the heat of the day but the meal and the wine tasting had taken its toll. A walk around the heritage site and gardens in an attempt to shake off the lethargy had finished them off. They could hardly put one foot in front of the other.

"Martin, can I sleep in here with you tonight?"

"If you want to but are you sure it's the best way forward?"

"Yes, I'm just scared I'll have another bad dream."

"OK."

She lay on the bed beside him, her head resting on his chest, he wrapped his arm around her shoulders and together, they drifted off to sleep.

Martin awoke to find Jo propped up on an elbow looking at him, the moonlight silhouetting her long hair as it fell around her shoulders.

"Martin, those men in the village, they really hurt me, not just physically but mentally as well. I'm afraid, afraid that I will never be able to live a normal life, with a husband and children, afraid of what I will do if someone touches me."

Martin reached over and gently laid his hand upon her outstretched arm.

"There's no need to be afraid, it may take time but it will sort itself out, the memories will fade, become less painful."

She looked into his eyes and said,

"Will you make love to me?"

He was startled, had he misheard her?

"Pardon?"

"Will you make love to me?"

"Oh, I don't think that would be a good idea."

"Why not, don't you like me?"

"Of course I like you, probably more than you think I do but it wouldn't be right. And I can think of at least three reasons why."

"What reasons?"

"Well, you're a vulnerable young lady who has suffered a great trauma for one and it might be seen as taking advantage. Two, I'm old enough to be your father. Three, your father would probably shoot me if I did and funnily enough, Dr Dhal asked me if my thoughts of you were of a sexual nature and I told her no."

"That's four and none of them are a good enough excuse! I won't tell Pa, or Ma for that matter. Plenty of older men have younger partners. Yes, I might still be vulnerable but I know what I have asked. I want, no, I need to feel like a woman again and I want you to make me that woman. I trust you to handle me with care, to help me banish my demons. I know you care for me why else would you fly thousands of miles to come and find me, why else would you visit my shrink to help her understand me? You know the ordeal I suffered, more I think than I do myself, that memory has still to be unlocked and I want someone that understands that to be with me when it does."

"Oh Jo, I understand your reasons but it feels wrong. I came here to help you not to take advantage."

She burst into tears.

"But you will be helping me, helping me to regain myself, to be the woman I once was, please, please help me."

Martin cradled her in his arms, her tears running down his chest, her body heaving with every sob, he kissed her cheek, tasting the saltiness of her tears.

She looked up at him, the moisture in her eyes glinting in the moonlight, it was decision time and whatever he decided, he would have to face the consequences.

"I don't have any condoms."

"I do, I bought some earlier."

"You little minx. How long have you been planning this? I get the feeling I've been ambushed."

"Only this evening, I bought them from a machine when we came back."

She lay beside him; a pleading look in her eyes.

He was unsure of how to proceed, this wasn't casual sex, it would be with someone he cared for but also someone he didn't look on as a sexual partner.

"Wait a moment," he said.

Jo felt him get off the bed and heard him go into the bathroom, thirty seconds later he sat beside her on the bed.

"Turn on to your stomach."

"Why?"

"You'll soon find out."

She rolled over, he moved and knelt in the space that she had left.

She felt a strange sensation on her back and shoulders, as if she was being touched by a feather but it was so light and almost cold.

Then he placed his hands on her shoulders and moved them in a circular motion, his thumbs rubbing into the nape of her neck easing the knotted muscle.

His movements although firm were not dragging on her skin, she realised what that feathery sensation had been caused by. Talcum powder.

He slowly worked his way down to the tip of her toes, stopping occasionally to dust her body with more talcum.

She could feel the tenseness in her muscles abating.

"OK, turn over. Close your eyes and relax."

She smelled the talcum as he dusted her chest, opening her eyes briefly to watch, it looked like he was in the act of frosting a cake.

His began at her shoulders again, kneading the muscle of her arms before applying a gentle circular motion to her torso, not touching her breasts at all. All the way down her tanned legs, dusting with talcum when needed.

He stopped, she felt him reposition himself and then felt his hands either side of her head, alternating between light feathery touch and firm pressure he massaged her head and neck, '*Pure bliss,*' she thought.

He stopped, she felt his body close to hers, a light kiss to her lips and then her throat, his hands caressing her breasts, tweaking her erect nipples playfully between his thumbs and forefingers, a lingering kiss to the nipples before continuing on down to her belly.

She felt his hot breath between her thighs and felt the tip of his tongue as it probed and caressed her most intimate of places.

Her nerve endings sent shock waves of delight through her body, shock waves that she had thought she might never experience again, given the injuries that she had suffered.

She moaned in pleasure, her hips rising, wanting, and needing greater pleasure.

She stretched out her hands and found his, grasping them firmly she pulled them to her breasts, moulding and kneading them around her perfectly formed and pert mounds. Releasing her grip on his hands, she again stretched out and gripped his head, pulling him hard against her.

Wave after wave of pleasure coursed through her body, bordering almost on pain such was the intensity, finally reaching the point of no return, her juices flowed, Martin spluttered and twisted but she didn't let go; she couldn't such was the power of her orgasm but she needed more, she needed to feel him inside of her.

Releasing her grip on his head she pulled him up to her, she could smell the sweet aroma of her bodily juices on his face, he placed his hands around her face, kissing her firmly on the lips, his manhood sliding between her thighs.

A picture of such horror and reality flashed into her head, she pushed him away.

"No, no, I can't." she said, as she rolled onto her side, curling into a ball crying loudly, her body once more heaving and convulsing.

Martin sat beside her, gently stroking her exposed cheek, wiping away the tears.

"It's OK, you're safe," he said, "there's no one here to hurt you, it's just a bad memory. It will soon be gone."

Laying down beside her, he pulled the cover over them and with his arm around her heaving body, comforting her, she eventually fell asleep.

It was still not yet daybreak, Martin was aware of movement next to him; opening one eye, he saw Jo sitting cross legged on the bed.

"I'm so sorry, I didn't mean to treat you like that, it was amazing, wonderful and unbelievably sensuous and then I ruined it."

"It's OK, it will take time to shake off those bad memories but they will go."

"Yes, hopefully but I made you do something that you didn't want to do, then I let you down."

"Don't worry about it. I guess we can say it is part of your treatment."

Uncrossing her legs, she slid into the bed and lay alongside of him, she kissed him fleetingly on the lips.

"I'm so glad you were there to help me. Earlier, when I pushed you away, I had a picture in my head of several black men holding me down and being forced upon. Is that what happened? I was terrified."

"Unfortunately it was, you were in a sorry state when I found you. If I hadn't got you out when I did, I doubt you would have survived. I'm glad that I was there to save you. I guess it was due to a certain part of my anatomy touching yours that brought back the memory. I'm sorry for that."

She reached under the cover and grasped him in her hand, feeling his manhood grow, she massaged it as it stiffened. She felt Martin's body tense and felt his hot sticky fluid pulse through her fingers, holding it firmly until it lay still.

She pulled his face to hers and kissed him long and fully on the lips.

"You deserved better than that but I hope you liked it."

He kissed her back, holding her tightly.

"You have just made this old man very happy," he said with a smile, "but I think I need a shower now."

Chapter 27

Their last full day in Cape Town, so much still to see.

"Martin, I've been thinking, I would like to do what Margarette does."

"You mean run a shop in Cape Town?"

"No silly, a charity for abused women."

"A good idea but I doubt you would need it in Steytlerville, Willowmore possibly. You could always ask Dr Dhal, she might have some ideas or know of someone who could help or even needs help to run a charity."

"I've booked a sunset champagne cruise for tonight and I thought we could go on a hop-on hop-off city tour before that. If that's OK with you? We can get some last minute-shopping and stop for a spot of lunch."

"Sounds good to me, I just need to avoid the crowds."

The sunset cruise was the ideal end to their visit, Martin had booked the cruise and meal package. After watching the sun go down over the Atlantic, the lights of Cape Town and the coast from a boat out in the bay, they shared a candlelit three course meal in a restaurant on the V and A waterfront, before catching a taxi back to the hotel.

A few final glasses of wine as they sat on the hotel terrace watching the stars, a cool night-time breeze ruffling the furled umbrellas and table cloths.

"A perfect way to end a perfect day. A toast," said Martin, "to friends, lovers and everyone else we know."

"Couldn't have said it better myself."

That night Jo didn't ask, she just climbed in to Martin's bed and was waiting for him when he emerged from the bathroom.

"Oh, have I got to sleep in the other room?" he asked.

"Only if you want a full night's sleep."

Not wanting to upset Jo, he climbed in beside her.

She was not troubled by scenes of horror as together, they made it a night of unbridled passion; at Martin's suggestion, Jo climbed on top.

"That way you can control when and how," he told her.

Jo wholeheartedly took his advice.

Chapter 28

"I hope you can drive. I'm worn out. I might have to stop halfway for a rest," Martin joked as they drove out of the hotel courtyard the next morning.

As they drove into the farmyard, Jo's Ma came out of the house and embraced her daughter pulling her close and kissing her on both cheeks.

"Why Ma, what's this for?"

"Nothing special, I'm just glad you're back, I was afraid I wouldn't see you again. I guess your ordeal haunts me as well."

"Don't worry, I won't be leaving again. I think I have lost my wanderlust. Where's Pa?"

"He went to the sheep, should have been back by now though. I've no doubt he will be along soon, his stomach will make sure of that."

They laughed. Jo's Pa liked his food.

Martin unloaded the car, carrying everything into Jo's room, his own gear would be placed in his room later.

Coming into the lounge, he saw a look of concern on the women's faces.

"What's wrong?" he asked.

"Pa is late, it's nearly dark and he is still not home. That's not like him at all."

"OK, why don't I go and look for him, he showed me his grazing land before we went away so I should be able to locate him. I'll tell him his dinner is getting cold!"

"I'll come with you," said Jo, "the quad carries two."

Driving along the bumpy, uneven track was slow going, Martin didn't want to risk Jo falling off.

They reached a high point and stopped to look for her Pa. He was nowhere to be seen.

Switching off the quad's engine, Martin strained his ears for any sound.

"Nothing other than the occasional bleating of sheep."

"Johann." he called loudly.

"Pa, where are you?" Jo joined in. No reply.

"Call the dogs Jo, they must be with your Pa."

"Max, Samson," she called several times.

They heard barking, it appeared to be coming from a low area of ground to the left of them, she called again and this time a dog appeared, coming out from behind a rocky outcrop.

Martin fired up the quad and drove as fast as possible towards the dog.

"It's Samson," Jo yelled in his ear, as they got closer.

They pulled up short of the dog, Samson growled as Martin dismounted and walked towards it.

"Jo, can you make sure Samson doesn't bite me, he doesn't look very friendly."

"Samson, come here boy, good dog. OK, I've got him."

Climbing over and then around the rocks, Martin at first saw Max standing upright, his eyes following Martin's every move.

Oh god, Johann was lying on the rocks below, motionless, his right arm at a funny angle and what appeared to be blood around his temple region.

"Jo, you'd better come and help, your Pa is hurt! And Max doesn't look to friendly either."

Samson beat Jo to the scene of the accident. Martin, still wary of the dogs was the last on the scene but was the first to examine Johann.

"He's breathing but unconscious, looks like he took a nasty blow to the head and his arm is, I think, dislocated."

Jo knelt beside her Pa, her nurses' training instantly kicking in. Carefully examining his head wound, she said.

"He needs to go to hospital urgently and I need some bandages and a sling."

Martin took off his shirt and tore it into strips.

"Here use this. Stay here with your Pa, I'll go and get help."

"Be quick, please."

Martin drove as fast as he could, wrestling with the steering as the rocky terrain tried to tear the handlebars from his grip.

Pulling up in the farmyard, he shouted,

"Anika, get an ambulance, Johann's had an accident."

Dashing into Johann's workshop, he gathered the items that he needed, as he placed them on the quad's load carrier, Anika came from the house.

"What has happened? I have called an ambulance but it will take time to get here."

"It looks like Johann fell, he has hit his head and damaged his arm, Jo, sorry Johanna, is with him. Is there anyone you can call to help? It will be difficult to get him back here."

"I will call some of the neighbours."

"OK, we are over the far side towards the river, if I leave the quad's lights on, it will help whoever to find us. Oh, and do you have a large torch or something similar that I can take, it's getting very dark and can I have two of those packets dried beans, the ones in sackcloth bags?"

He took the large handheld lamp and sacks of beans, placed them in the carrier and headed off towards Jo and her Pa.

Scrambling down to Jo, he set the lamp on a suitable rock, it lit up the area perfectly.

He then climbed back to the quad, gathered most of the items and climbing back down, laid them beside Jo.

"One more item to get," he said, as he disappeared again.

Jo heard a scraping sound from above and then Martin telling her to keep her head down. Moments later, a wardrobe door attached to a rope, slid down the rock beside her.

Martin climbed down beside her, she had bandaged her Pa's head and arranged his arm ready for a sling.

"I couldn't find a sling but I thought this would do," he said pulling off a length of adhesive fabric tape, "we can bind his arm in place."

Jo looked at him.

"Sure that will work but what is that for?" pointing to the wardrobe door.

"Right! Trying to get your Pa out of here will be difficult, so I thought we could strap or at least tape him to this door and then using the quad and brute strength, pull and push him up and over the rocks."

"And the beans?"

"To stop his head from moving, we can tape a bag either side of his head, just in case he has a spinal injury, yes?"

"Your Ma has called an ambulance but she said it will take a while, she is also calling for some neighbourly help."

Getting Johann onto the door was no easy task, they had to be careful not to damage his arm any further and Jo had to hold his head steady at all times when they moved him.

The adhesive tape strapped him firmly in place, the bean bags, one either side of his head were also taped to the door with the tape extending across his chin and forehead.

"OK, I think that will do. Jo, if you connect the rope end to the trailer hitch on the quad, drive forward until you take up the slack and then yell, I'll lift from down here and hopefully we can get your Pa out."

Jo yelled, Martin heaved but it did not move far. Martin could hear the quad's wheels spinning.

"Hold it, I'm coming up."

Martin thought he heard voices, looking up he saw a man's face peering down at him from the rocks above followed by the face of another older man.

"Hej, ons het kom help." said the younger of them.

"Sorry, can you say that in English?"

"Oh yes, we have come to help."

The dogs growled ominously, the older of the men called out to them.

"Hej Max, Samson kom hier, goeie honde."[13]

Both dogs ran to him.

With Martin and the younger of the two helpers lifting the door to which Johann was strapped and Jo and the older man riding the quad, they managed to lift their injured cargo to safety.

They carefully lifted the door and laid it across the carrier of one of the quads, tying it securely.

Jo steered her precious cargo slowly and carefully with Martin and the older man walking either side of the door back down to the farmyard.

The younger of the two helpers driving the other quad.

Max and Samson, ever alert for predators, trailed behind, their eyes shining like jewels when caught in the rear lights of the quads.

The ambulance was turning into the farmyard as the rescue party reached it. Anika, tears streaming down her face rushed over to her husband, still lying unconscious on the door.

_____

[13] Come here, good dogs

Jo parked by the ambulance, Martin untied the rope and cut through the adhesive tape that was holding Johann.

The paramedics brought out their stretcher and backboard, carefully transferred Johann and loaded him into the ambulance, in order to carry out a further examination.

"He needs urgent specialist care," one of them pronounced. "Who will come with him?"

Anika looked at Jo.

"You go with him Ma, I'll follow in the truck."

"We'll follow in the truck, just in case any help is needed," added Martin. "Don't worry we'll sort things out."

The ambulance set off down the track, red lights flashing, vividly lighting the sparse bush as it went.

Chapter 29

Jo went into the house to collect a few items that her parents might need, Martin thanked the two helpers, who turned out to be the nearest neighbours, Hendrik van der Tuin and his son Pieter.

They were driving away as Jo, carrying a bulging bag came out of the house, locking the front door after closing it.

"The dogs are loose, I've locked the house, can we go?"

They could see the glow of the red lights in the distance as Martin broke the speed limits to get to the hospital.

By the time they had parked and made their way to the emergency department, Johann was lying on a trolley surrounded by medics.

Anika, as white as a sheet was being comforted by a nurse. On seeing Jo, she ran forward and clung to her tightly.

"They say it is bad, the paramedic had him connected to machines in the ambulance and was very concerned. They suspect a 'depressed skull fracture'. Is that bad?"

"Don't worry Ma, it can be fixed."

A nurse showed them to the relatives' waiting room.

"A doctor will come and see you soon," she said, "there are refreshments down the corridor." Then she left.

The doctor knocked on the door, opened it, poked his head around and asked, "de Klerk?"

"Yes."

"I'm Doctor Tao. I have examined Mr de Klerk. He has a depressed open fracture to the right temple area, a dislocated right shoulder and a fracture to his right clavicle.

The most serious is the skull fracture, a CT scan shows the area of damage and we have taken your husband," looking at Anika, "to the operating theatre. It will be a while before we can see the results.

176

The other damage will be dealt with after. A nurse will ask you some questions and help you with some forms that need to be filled in."

Anika looked very frail, she was struggling to remain calm and composed, Jo comforted her by cradling her Ma's head against her shoulder.

"Don't worry Ma. They will soon have Pa back on his feet." Although she might have sounded positive, her look said otherwise.

"We might be here some time, perhaps you should go back to the farm Martin. I will call you when we know more."

"I can wait, I'm not going to leave you stranded. If nothing has changed by the morning, I'll go back, feed the dogs and check the sheep. Then come back, if that's alright with you."

It was a long night, the operation took three and a half hours but with the post-op waiting time, it was past four in the morning before they were told that the operation was completed.

The surgeons had removed the broken pieces of bone, cleaned the area and wired the pieces back in place before stitching the damaged skin together, so far the results were looking good, although infection was possible due to the time the wound was open.

Damage to the brain was also possible, only time would tell.

Johann had been placed in the critical care unit to recover. Anika and Jo were only allowed a quick bedside visit.

While Anika and Jo were with Johann, Martin searched for local accommodation. He booked a double room at the Royal Hotel, just down the road from the hospital. He would drop them off on his way back to the farm; if they needed to get to the hospital before he returned, it would only be a very short taxi ride.

"Thank you Martin but it is not necessary, I can wait here." Said Anika.

"No Ma, Martin is right, we can go to the hotel, rest and be ready for when Pa wakes up. You can't sit in this little room all day and they won't let you stay in the CCU."

Martin had to have his credit card swiped at the hotel reception and then he was off to the farm.

"Call me on the mobile if anything changes and I'll come straight back, otherwise, I'll be back later today when I've fed the animals and grabbed some sleep. You get some sleep too."

Max and Samson were waiting at the gate as he drove up, they must have recognised the truck and followed it to the house without making a fuss, it was only when Martin emerged from the cab that their senses came alert.

He walked slowly and purposefully to the house, expecting to hear the pounding of dogs' paws behind him and to feel teeth in his rear, thankfully it didn't happen.

First job on the list, feed the dogs, maybe they might be friendlier.

A few hours' sleep and he would be as right as rain.

Mobile plugged in to charge beside the bed, he was asleep as his head hit the pillow.

Martin was woken by the sound of dogs barking and a rapping on a door.

He rolled over and looked at the clock. Three fifteen.

"Oh hell!" He'd overslept.

The dogs were still barking and where was that knocking from? He groggily staggered to the front door.

"Sorry, I didn't mean to wake you." said Pieter. "I just came to find out how everybody was."

"Come in, I can spare a few minutes while I get myself together. Coffee?"

"Yes, thanks."

Martin relayed the information from the hospital, adding that Anika and Jo would be staying in Willowmore for a few days and that he would be travelling to and fro and looking after the farm,

"Not that I'm a farmer."

"I can help with the farm. It's what neighbours do out here. I'm not a farmer either but I did grow up on one, well, at least until my early teens."

"Thanks, I probably will need some help, I spent a little time with Johann but I wouldn't say I really took that much notice when it comes to feeding. Actually, I need to feed and water now before it gets dark. I have to go to the hospital later."

"Thanks Pieter, you've been a great help but I might have to call on you again."

"Oh you'll get used to it, luckily it's only a small flock now, years ago when Johanna and I were schoolkids, and the flocks were much bigger, mind you everybody had staff to look after them."

"You have known Jo a while then?"

"We used to go to school together, childhood sweethearts you might say."

"What changed that?"

"Ma and Pa divorced, I went to live in Pretoria, only coming back on odd occasions. Then hardly at all. University and a career in construction, I've been working in the Middle East for the last few years, took a break at the end of the contract, decided to visit Pa. Do you have a mobile?"

"Sure, why?"

"I'll give you my number, you can call if you need help."

"Thanks."

Letting the dogs loose, Martin climbed into the truck and headed to Willowmore. It was that time of day when the sinking sun left long shadows, and areas of almost complete darkness where it was shielded by hills and rocky outcrops, it was also the time of day when the wildlife ventured out in search of food and water.

He drove carefully and complied with the speed limits, fully alert this time, not like yesterday after just having driven from Cape Town.

He called Jo on her mobile, she and Anika were at the hospital.

He buzzed the intercom for the CCU, a nurse let him in as far as the nurses' station. Looking into the ward, he could see Jo and Anika standing by a bed, the patient lying flat surrounded by machines and laced with tubes and wires of various colours.

Jo looked up and beckoned him over.

Her face and that of her mother were stained in rivulets, what little make-up that they had applied had run in the salty liquid of their tears.

Johann was heavily sedated, much like Jo had been when Martin had last seen her last in Mozambique. His head was tightly bandaged, leaving only his face exposed and that was trailing tubes from his nose and mouth.

The rest of his body was covered in a thin sheet but tubes were visible exiting from under that also.

"How is he doing?"

Anika looked up, looked at Jo who answered,

"As well as can be expected, it's early days. They will keep him sedated for a few days, to allow his brain to recover. Hopefully, an infection will not take hold. He's on antibiotics just in case. His shoulder has been set and the break in the clavicle will mend in time. But it will take a long time for Pa to fully recover, that's for sure."

"Will just under three months be long enough?"

"Why?"

179

"Well, I was given a three-month visa on arrival, it's only had a couple of weeks used, so I can stay for a while to help out. If that's of any use!"

Jo couldn't resist, she grasped his face and kissed him on the lips.

"Oh Ma, did you hear that, Martin will stay and help us until Pa is better."

"Until the visa runs out, I don't know if it can be extended, I can ask nearer the time if I have to."

"Thank you Martin, we appreciate that." Anika replied.

Dropping Jo and Anika at the hotel very late that night, Martin drove back to the farm, he had a list of items to take back with him the following day.

Max and Samson greeted him with a perfunctory sniff as he climbed out of the truck and headed indoors for some well-earned sleep.

Sleep came quickly but daylight seemed to come just as fast.

Max and Samson were waiting patiently at the backdoor for their food, they seemed to have accepted Martin, '*Perhaps,*' he thought, '*it was because he was feeding them.*'

Before he did anything else, there was an important task to carry out, he took a business card from his wallet and dialled the number.

"Good morning Judith. It's Martin Newman, may I speak with Dr Dhal? It's important."

"Just a minute, Mr Newman, I'll see if she is free."

"Martin. How can I help?"

After a late breakfast, Martin decided to check on the sheep, Max and Samson trotted alongside the quad with him on it in the same manner that they did with Johann.

Farm work over for the morning, Martin left the dogs to roam free.

Taking the truck into town was an interesting experience, he was given some peculiar looks when some of the townsfolk after initially waving, realised that it wasn't Johann at the wheel.

The fuel station attendant was most put out when Martin pulled up with the fill point on the wrong side to the pump.

"Hej Martin."

He looked around,

Hendrik had spotted him and pulled alongside.

"How is Johann?"

"Hi Hendrik, he's been operated on, has a fractured skull and is in the critical care unit. Could be a while before he is back but hopefully he will fully recover."

"Pieter tells me you are looking after the farm."

"Yes."

"You need help, you call, OK."

"OK, thanks."

"Menheer de Klerk is injured?" The pump attendant, a short stocky African with a wizened face asked.

"Afraid so."

"How?"

"Not sure, he seems to have fallen and hit his head."

"Please, you tell him Jacob says to get well."

"I will, thank you."

Back at the farm, Martin decided to look at the site of the accident, to try and determine what had caused Johann to damage himself.

Pulling up, he could see the imprints of the quad tyres from the previous visits and the scrape marks of boots and the door.

He climbed down to where Johann had been laying, blood still stained the rock. He stood where he assumed Johann's feet would have been and looked around.

Nothing, then he noticed several small scrape marks on the face of the large rock in front of him, a tuft of wool was trapped in a crevice below, and more wool was below that.

'Well, it looks like he tried to get a sheep out of here,' thought Martin, *'he must have fallen after he got it free.'*

"Message to self, don't try to rescue sheep."

Back at the house, a quick meal, load up the items on the list before another trip to the hospital, it was a little early but the sheep had been fed and watered, it would be nice to drive in daylight.

"Hi Martin, you're early today."

"I woke up early, a farmer's work won't wait you know," he said with a wry smile. "Anyway, it paid dividends, I fed and watered the sheep earlier than before and decided to look at the area that we found your Pa, it looks like one of his sheep may have fallen down into the gulley and Pa was attempting to get it out when the accident occurred, I found scrape marks on the rocks and tufts of wool in the crevices."

"Oh, that sounds logical, Pa would not have left the animal trapped. It would be typical of him to try to get it out alone before calling for help."

"How is he?"

"As well as can be expected. The doctor told us that it will be a while before we know what damage, if any, has been done to his brain, apparently the right temple area or to be more correct the right 'Temporal Lobe' is involved with language and information processing, fortunately it is the non-dominant lobe in Pa, being that he is right handed and so hopefully any damage will be only minor. He may suffer from memory loss and difficulty with word association but we will see."

"We can only hope for the best; incidentally, Jacob at the petrol station sends his best wishes to your Pa for a speedy recovery."

"Hello Martin," said Anika as she returned to the relatives' room. "I trust Johanna has given you an update?"

"Yes thanks. How are you holding up?"

"As well as can be expected, I hope you brought those clothes I asked for, these ones need a wash."

"Everything is in the car. Do you want them now?"

"No, later when we go to the hotel will be fine, are you coming to the ward?"

They had only just arrived Johann's bed when, unseen until almost within touching distance, Dr Dhal appeared.

"Hello Johanna, Anika, how is Johann?"

"How do you know about Pa?"

"No secrets around here. Perhaps we should go outside of the ward, the relatives' room would be best, they like to keep the ward quiet if possible."

"Would you like to tell me what happened?"

Between them, Jo and her Ma told the doctor of the incident from Johann not returning for dinner right up to being taken to the operating theatre. Both bursting into tears at various stages of describing the events.

Martin remained quiet.

Dr Dhal listened, not saying a word until they finished.

"Well, I can tell you that Johann is in capable hands and although his recovery may take a while it hopefully will become just a distant memory, one of life's little adventures. If any of you need my help whilst you are here, you know where my office is."

Looking at her watch she said,

"Sorry, must go, I have a meeting in ten minutes."

"Martin, Ma and I have been discussing you, more to the point, your situation. We really appreciate what you are doing for us but we don't think it is right that you should be looking after the farm and then driving here every day."

"You must be worn out and very tired, plus it's not safe to drive at night what with the poor driving of some people and the wild animals, if you had an accident we would be devastated to say the least. We would be happy for you not to come here for a few days. You're not a farmer and it must be quite a challenge just to fill Pa's boots, let alone travel here as well. It's not that we don't want to see you, it's more like we don't want to lose you."

"Okay, I get the point but I have been offered help on the farm if I need it. Pieter has offered to help any time I need it and Hendrik stopped at the filling station and told me the same."

"Pieter?"

"Yes, Hendrik's son, you know, he helped get your Pa up from the rocks."

"That was Pieter! Oh my god, I never realised. I'm so sorry, please tell him."

"I will. He told me that you and he used to be sweethearts! But then his parents split up and he went off to Pretoria."

Jo blushed.

"You could say that. I haven't seen him for ages, he visited his Pa very infrequently and then I would often be away when he did come."

"Well, he was obviously pleased to see you. I could tell by the way he spoke about you. Anyway, between the three of us, the farm will be well looked after. Even Max and Samson seem to accept me, although that might be because they associate me with food. But, if it makes you both happy I will restrict my visits and only come when requested. Now, I think it's time for me to see Johann if possible."

Johann was still lying comatose on the bed as before, a spaghetti-like bundle of wires and tubes plugged into various bleeping, light flashing machines.

"He is breathing normally," a nurse told Martin when he asked, "his stats are all regular, we are keeping him sedated to allow his brain to recover. The doctor will tell you more."

Watching him lying there, unable to communicate was a pitiful sight. He could only imagine the anguish Jo and Anika were going through. He had only seen Jo for a couple of days in that same state at the UMA hospital but that had been torture.

Driving back to the farm that evening was a bittersweet event, he understood their motives for his not visiting the hospital but it didn't stop him from feeling that he should be with them; Jo had at least agreed to call with updates on her Pa's condition.

Arriving earlier than on previous nights, he allowed himself a couple of beers whilst sitting on the stoep, the night sky was crystal clear, millions of stars twinkling above, the only sounds were those of nature, perfect, except for the damned mosquitoes.

Chapter 30

'Morning, no need to rush,' he thought. Hell, I'm awake, I may as well get up.

A leisurely breakfast was interrupted by the barking of Max and Samson, they were still loose in the farmyard.

From the front doorway, Martin could see Pieter out of his car standing by the farmyard gate.

"Hej Martin, call off the dogs, I have come to help."

"Max, Samson, come here boys." He led them around to their pen for food, allowing Pieter to pull into the farmyard and enter the house.

"Mevrou [14] de Klerk, called Pa this morning, told him that you would be working the farm until Menheer is back and could he look after you. Pa told her that from what he had seen you didn't need looking after but yes he would help if needed. So, he sent me to see if you needed help."

"Thanks, I was wondering where to start, Johann was always busy but I'm not sure what he was doing, I went out to the fields with him to feed and water the sheep but that was about it. I guess there's fence mending and equipment repairs to carry out, that was to be my starting point."

Together, they worked through the morning and into the late afternoon, probably carrying out tasks that not necessarily needed doing at that time but would have done in the near future.

The fences were all good, no need to be in the hot sun, so most of the work was carried out in the shade of the barns.

A camaraderie developed between them. Jo being the focal point of their discussions. Pieter was anxious to find out the relationship between Martin and Jo, whilst trying rather badly to disguise the questions.

Martin, sensing that Pieter's questioning was more than just general interest, answered guardedly, not wanting to upset either Jo or Pieter. If there was to be a

---

[14] Mrs/Madam de Klerk

relationship between the two of them, it had to be of their making. Martin did not want to act as cupid.

He gave only the briefest of details of his and Jo's time in Mozambique, skipping over the most horrific parts, instead describing in greater depth the finds in the cave, the boarding of the bus and of Jo's courage in killing the snake.

"Wow! That must have been a hell of a trip."

"I'll let Jo tell you the full story." Was all Martin would say.

As Pieter was leaving, he asked Martin the question that had been lurking in the back of his mind all day.

"Martin, can I ask, are you and Johanna involved, romantically, I mean?"

Martin had anticipated this and was prepared.

"Involved? Yes. Romantically? Probably not as you imagine. I have feelings for Jo, of course, but I am far too old to be a suitor, she needs someone more of her own age, someone who will grow old with her, give her the lifestyle and children she deserves.

But, all that needs to be addressed in the future, she is still in a very vulnerable state not only because of her ordeal in Mozambique but because of what has happened to her Pa and I will do whatever is necessary to ensure that nothing hurts her or her recovery."

Those next few days passed quickly enough, a rhythm had been found, Pieter's teenage experience as a farmer's son, albeit many years previous smoothed the path, showing Martin ways to carry out tasks in half the time.

Late afternoon of the third day, tasks finished they sat on the stoop with some cold beers, talk once again was of Jo.

"Has Johanna ever mentioned me?" Pieter asked.

"Not to me."

"Oh."

"But then she has had a lot of problems to contend with, the details that I gave you of our time in Mozambique were an abridged version, it was far more horrific than you could possibly imagine, so much so that even I have had nightmares about it.

Jo attends a clinic to help her through her ordeal, she suffers nightmares as well, only far more frequent and unpleasant than mine. She also suffers from memory loss, mainly related to her ordeal but it probably includes earlier memories."

"Will she fully recover?"

"I believe so, the doctors seem confident, it will just take time."

"Certain events, sounds, places even seem to trigger memory recall, not all good I might add.

We were in Cape Town a few days ago, a group of black youths came our way, not aggressively but Jo had a meltdown; conversely her Pa showed her a story in a newspaper about a cave find in Mozambique and her memory bounced back with all the details.

So yes, she will, I think recover, she just needs time and care."

Pieter had left for home; the dogs had been let out for night and once again, Martin was star-gazing. The phone rang.

"Hello."

"Martin."

"Hi Jo, how is everything?"

"Pa is awake, he recognised us."

"That's great news."

"It is. It most certainly is."

"The doctor says that he should be able to leave the CCU for a normal ward if all goes well in the next day or so. There are no signs of infection and the wound is healing well."

"That's wonderful. You and your Ma must be really pleased."

"We are."

"How are things otherwise, are you OK for money and does the hotel still have rooms available for your stay?"

"Yes and yes. How are your farming skills?"

"Great. You won't recognise the place, I've bought some cows, goats and chickens and the wheat is six foot high."

"Now I'm worried."

"No need, I am only joking. The farm is fine, as am I, Pieter comes and helps. He seems a nice chap, likes you a lot. Always asks if you have called. Actually, that's probably why he comes round."

"Hopefully we will all be home fairly soon, although Pa will probably not be able to work for a while, so we will need you around."

"No problem, like I said before, my three months are not up yet."

"You made that sound like a prison sentence."

"Oh, far from it, I'm actually enjoying myself. Do you want me to bring you anything?"

"No thanks, we have everything we need. Dr Dhal, came around earlier, she is a breath of fresh air, helps both Ma and me. I don't know what she told Pa's medical team but they really go out of their way to keep us informed and give us access to Pa whenever we want."

"Great, give your Pa, my regards, tell him I need someone to show me the ropes."

"I thought Pieter was doing that!"

"He is, just no need to let on, it might give him a big head."

"OK, must go, will call again soon. Bye."

Chapter 31

"Hello, de Klerk farm."

"Hi Martin, that was very formal."

"Hi Jo, you usually call on the mobile, so given it was the house phone I thought I had better make a good impression, it might have been the bank manager."

"Oh, you are funny."

"Hopefully, Pa will be allowed home tomorrow, the doctor will make a decision after his morning visit."

"That's great."

"We can only hope. He will be under strict instructions not to go out into the bush, no physical labour and plenty of rest. I've told them that we have capable staff to carry out all of the farm work and Pa will be given plenty of rest."

"Staff! What staff!"

"Why you, of course."

"Careful, I might ask for a pay rise."

"Ha ha, seeing that you work for free, you can have as big a rise as you like."

"Hmm, I walked right into that one. If you call as soon as you get the all clear, I'll come and get you."

"OK, I expect it will be after midday, they do their rounds from 9 till 12. If they let Pa out, I'll go back to the hotel, check out and bring everything to the hospital. It will be less hassle in the long run."

"Sounds good to me. I guess I had better tidy up, don't want your Ma bending my ear."

"Why is it I don't believe you, I've seen how tidy you are."

"Ouch, you know me too well."

"See you tomorrow, bye."

Martin sat on the stoep, ice cold beer in hand, mulling over the tasks for the next day.

Johann would still be in a fragile state, the farm truck although more than capable was not very comfortable, it was built for rough ground and Martin's hire car would be a little cramped for four people and baggage.

'Maybe,' he thought, '*Hendrik might know where he could get a bigger car for the day.*'

He dialled the number.

"Van der Tuin."

"Hi Hendrik, it's Martin Newman."

"Hello Martin, do you need help?"

"Yes but not physically, I might need to hire a large or at least, a comfortable car to pick up Johann from the hospital tomorrow. Johanna has called to tell me that hopefully, he will be allowed home tomorrow and I don't think the farm truck or my little car will be suitable."

"Ha, I don't know about you English, but here in South Africa, neighbours help each other, you can use my old Mercedes. It's comfortable and has space for all and their baggage."

"That will be great, thanks but I don't have a South African license nor insurance."

"No problem, Pieter will drive. It can seat five. I will get it ready tonight and if you need it just call. Ja."

"Yes, as soon as I hear anything I will call. Thanks."

Up early the next day, farm work finished, house tidied, Martin sat within earshot of the phone. Midday came and went.

He was just making a coffee when it rang, putting the cup down clumsily, he split most of it on the floor, blast, the clean-up can wait.

"Hello, de Klerk!"

"Hello Staff, can you pick us up?" giggled a voice down the phone.

"Madam's wish is my command." he answered. "The driver will be with you in about two hours."

"Oh Martin, you sound so serious."

"It's serious business, don't you know, transporting valuable cargo." He laughed, "OK, see you soon."

"Van der Tuin."

"Hi Hendrik, Johann is ready to leave the hospital."

"I will send Pieter to collect you."

"No need, please ask Pieter to go directly to the hospital, I will call Johanna and arrange for her to meet him at the main entrance. There will be more room in the car without me."

"Yes, good idea, Pieter will be leaving in a few minutes."

"Thanks, bye."

Making note of the time, Martin made another cup of coffee, cleaned up the spillage and sat out on the stoep.

One and a half hours after his phone call to Hendrik, Martin called Johanna. She answered on the first ring.

"Martin."

"The driver should be pulling in to the car park very soon. He is a handsome young chap, blue eyes, blond hair and driving his father's Mercedes."

"Pieter?"

"Yes, I thought you might need something more comfortable than the truck, Hendrik offered his Merc but I couldn't legally drive it. See you soon and tell him to drive carefully. Bye."

Max and Samson heard the crunch of tyres on the gravel track, alerting Martin to the arrival of a cream Mercedes Estate. It pulled to a stop at the bottom of the stoep steps.

Jo and her Ma eased Johann carefully from the rear seat of the car and guided him into the house, while Martin and Pieter followed with the baggage.

Martin heard a raised voice of complaint from Johann.

"I have been inside for days. I want to sit outside and enjoy the sunset."

Johann still in the clutches of his wife and daughter came out onto the stoep and was placed in his favourite chair.

"Thank you, now I am at home."

Pieter, stood by the driver's door of the Mercedes, just grinned.

"I sure my Pa would be the same." He said.

As he turned to get into the car, Jo walked over to him and kissed him on both cheeks, he went bright red with embarrassment.

"Now look what you've done," said Martin. "Embarrassing the staff, disgraceful behaviour."

Jo looked at him.

"Are you jealous?" She asked.

"I believe I told you before, you're a little minx." He said, grinning.

Their banter was lost on everyone else.

191

Chapter 32

Martin was roused from his slumber by noises from somewhere in the house, it took a few seconds for him to recollect his thoughts and remember that he was no longer alone.

Opening the bedroom door, he was greeted with the smell of freshly brewed coffee and the sounds of cups being placed on a table.

Anika was holding a cup to her lips when he entered the kitchen.

"Sorry Martin, did I wake you?" she asked.

"No," he lied, "I was awake. Any chance of some coffee?"

"Help yourself, I will take some to Johann, he has not had a good night, to be expected I suppose."

"Yes, I guess it will be difficult for a while but I will stay and help on the farm until he is fit and well and with Johanna and Pieter's help, I will keep the farm running as Johann would like and allow you to concentrate on his recovery."

Returning from the bush having checked the flock and filled the water troughs, Martin was surprised to see Hendrik's truck in the farmyard, he was even more surprised to see not Hendrik but Pieter sitting at the kitchen table, drinking coffee and talking animatedly to Jo.

They looked up as he walked in.

"Hi Martin, would you like some coffee?" asked Jo, adding, "Pieter and I have been reliving old times, they seem so long ago."

"That's okay, I will help myself, I really need something to eat, smells like your ma has been baking, hope there's something left?"

The days passed and turned into weeks, a routine had been established.

Martin looked after the farm, with occasional help from Pieter, Anika concentrated on Johann's recovery and Jo took on the household duties.

Pieter was a frequent visitor to the farm but he spent more time with Jo than actually helping with farm chores; although if asked he was always ready to assist, he would eagerly accompany Jo to town and even accompanied her to the hospital for her regular appointment with Dr Dhal.

But all was not well. Martin sensed a storm on the horizon. Johann was becoming very difficult, belligerent even and Anika was often teary eyed.

Returning from feeding the animals one afternoon, Martin was surprised not to see Pieter's truck in the farmyard.

Walking into the house, he could hear Anika sobbing loudly and Jo trying vainly to console her.

"What's the matter? Where's Pieter?"

"It's Pa, he and Ma have had an argument, a really bad argument and he said some terrible things. I sent Pieter home."

"Where is your Pa?"

"In the bedroom."

Martin walked down the corridor to Jo's parents' room. Knocking loudly on the door he said.

"Johann, it's Martin, may I come in?"

"Martin wie?" (Who)

"Martin Newman!"

"Ek ken jou nie, gaan weg."[15]

Martin opened the door to find himself confronted by a very irate Johann, holding an over and under shotgun in his hands.

"It's okay Johann, I mean you no harm, put the gun down please."

"Gaan weg, anders skiet ek jou."[16] Johann shouted as he advanced towards the doorway.

Martin backed into the corridor followed by Johann.

Jo, hearing the commotion appeared at the far end of the corridor.

"Pa sit die geweer neer."[17]

Johann turned towards her, the shotgun now pointing her way. Fearing the worst, Martin lunged at him grasping the barrel, forcing it upwards and pushing Johann back into the bedroom, the momentum caused Johann's finger to squeeze the trigger, a blast of lead pellets blew away the top of the door frame and the wall above it, the sound was deafening.

---

[15] I do not know you, go away

[16] Go away or I will shoot you

[17] "Pa" put the gun down

As they fell to the floor, Johann squeezed the trigger again firing the other barrel which by now was close to Martin's left ear. The pellets had blasted a hole in the ceiling and penetrated the roof, shafts of daylight filtered through the tin roofing illuminated the roof space. The bedroom was enveloped in a thick haze.

Martin staggered to his feet, his hearing gone, he felt sick but he was now holding the shotgun.

Johann lay on the floor, staring vacantly at the ceiling.

Anika rushed into the room, closely followed by Jo.

Surveying the carnage but finding both men alive was an obvious relief. Anika far from being sympathetic to Johann's plight, castigated him for his stupidity.

Jo, however, had sat Martin down in a chair in order to attend to his wounds, his left ear and scalp had been nicked by the flying pellets and were bleeding freely.

Martin was dazed, he was having difficulty processing the event although he knew what had happened. It was all a blur.

What he did know, however, was that his ear felt wet and was throbbing and that he couldn't hear properly.

As they were coming out of the corridor heading towards the kitchen, Pieter burst through the front door.

"Is everything okay? I heard shots."

He saw Martin's bandaged head.

"Oh my God! What happened?"

Silence for a few seconds then Martin said,

"A little accident, Johann was showing me his shotgun, I didn't know it was loaded and when I went to grasp it, it went off."

"Twice? I heard two shots!"

"Unfortunately, Johann's finger got stuck in the guard."

Pieter looked at Jo and then Anika for another explanation.

They just looked back.

"How bad is your wound?"

"Just a scratch and I seem to have lost my hearing in this ear," pointing to his bandaged head, "but I have had a wonderful nurse attend to it."

Pieter looked down the corridor, seeing the debris he walked to the bedroom door.

"Good grief! It's a wonder someone wasn't killed. It will be a lot of work to sort this out."

Looking at Jo he asked,

"Are you sure this was an accident?"

"Yes!" She replied emphatically.

"We will clean up the mess and it won't look half as bad."

"I'll help you."

"No need. We can manage. I sure we all appreciate your concern and your coming over but we are OK."

Pieter took the hint.

"OK, I'll be off, call me if you need anything."

He left the way he came in and sped out of the farmyard, leaving a cloud of dust in his wake.

"Johanna, that was very rude."

"Sorry Ma but I didn't want him asking questions, I think it will be best if no one else gets involved."

Martin and Johann were sat on the sofa, both with bandaged heads looking sorry for themselves, although for different reasons.

Jo was concerned, Martin looked very pale and was obviously in pain, her Pa just looked bewildered.

Martin assured her that apart from a splitting headache and throbbing ear, he was fine.

"Johanna, help me clear this mess."

"Coming Ma."

It took several hours for them to clear up and temporarily patch the holes in the ceiling, the damage to the roof could wait.

Jo and Anika kept a watchful eye on the two men whilst walking to and fro removing the debris.

They were in the final stages of the clean up when Anika heard Johann's voice.

"Martin, what happened? Why are you bandaged up?"

"Oh, a minor mishap, your shotgun went off as you handed it to me."

"My shotgun?"

"Yes, don't you remember sitting in your bedroom with it?"

Johann's face paled, the shock of reality suddenly apparent.

"Oh my God! Did I do that to you?"

"It was an accident. Like I said, the gun went off as you handed it to me."

Jo and Anika, their task finished, came back into the lounge.

"Come, Johann, sit on the stoep, I'll fetch you a beer."

"What about Martin?"

"He's OK. Pa, I need to check his wound." said Jo.

Sitting next to Martin on the sofa, Jo looked at the bandage covering Martin's ear. The blood had seeped through but it was tinged with a straw coloured fluid.

"I'm going to change your dressing Martin, it's a little soiled."

"OK."

Her suspicions were right, fluid was leaking from the ear canal, probably due to a burst eardrum.

"I'll bandage you up again but you need hospital treatment."

"Why?"

"It looks as though your eardrum has burst, loud noises can do that."

"But they will want to know how and the pellets will have left their mark."

"Not only the pellets, the blast also. We will have to stick to the story that you told Pieter."

"Yes, probably the best way, we need to keep your Pa out of this as much as possible but do I really need hospital treatment?"

"Afraid so. We could try Dr Jacobson, our local physician but I think he would say the same thing and that would add another person into the loop."

"OK," he sighed, "will you drive me there?"

"Of course and I'll bring you back."

"Ma, I'm taking Martin to the hospital."

"Why? I thought you said the wound wasn't too bad."

"The wound is small but it looks as though he's burst an eardrum and that needs medical attention."

"Won't they ask questions?"

"I expect so, we will keep to the story and if anyone comes before we get back, you keep to what we told Pieter earlier."

"What if someone asks why your Pa had the gun out?"

"Tell them he was going to shoot rats."

Chapter 33

They only had a short wait at the hospital's accident department.

It was confirmed that Martin's eardrum was perforated, the good news was that it would most likely heal with no side effects although his hearing would be affected until that time; the bad news was that it could take several weeks and until it was fully healed, he was not to get it wet, go diving or fly.

His scalp and ear tissue damage would heal quite quickly and although the missing top of his ear would never regrow, his hair would.

Questions were asked as to the origin of the damage, all firearm wounds are reportable they were told. Thankfully, the administrator and doctor agreed that it was an unfortunate accident and given that Martin was a foreigner and paid cash, embarrassing questions were dispensed with.

Driving back to the farm, Jo said,

"You saved my life again, didn't you?"

"I don't know, I saw your Pa swing the shotgun towards you and I just acted out of instinct, I didn't even know if it was loaded or even if he would have fired, it all happened so quickly."

They sat in silence for a good few kilometres until Jo said,

"Do you think I was rude to Pieter?"

"Not rude, just firm. You did the right thing. The last thing we need is for the police to get involved and I guess that's what would happen if the truth got out."

"Will he forgive me?"

"I think so. He is undoubtedly in love with you, so I'm sure apart from a little wounded pride, he will be back tomorrow."

"In love with me?"

"Oh yes, hopelessly so. I'm surprised you didn't realise. You only have to look at the amount of time that he spends with you when he comes to the farm instead of helping me."

"I thought you didn't need help."

"True but that doesn't stop him coming. He seems a nice young man, ideally suited to a young lady such as yourself."

"You're not jealous?"

"Of course not. I'm far too old to be your suitor. You need someone your own age and background, not some old fart who's ready for his slippers and pipe to be brought to him."

"I thought you liked me."

"I do, more than you can imagine but I am too old for you and I cannot give you the one thing that couples desire most; children. My marriage fell apart for that very reason and I would not want to go through that scenario again, nor put anyone else that I loved in that predicament."

"Oh Martin, I'm so sorry."

"Don't be sorry for me, life sometimes throws a curved ball, you just have to run with it. I hope I have not been giving you false hope. I came here out of genuine concern for your well-being, not to seduce you with my charm. If this leaves you feeling uncomfortable, then I will return to the UK sooner."

"Don't be silly, of course I don't want you to go. I appreciate your telling me this. You have helped me get my life back as well as possibly saving it again, I might add. Besides, the doctor said you cannot fly until you are healed, so you are stuck here with me."

"I will willingly stay as long as I can. However, we need to get your Pa fully up and running as soon as possible, I have an idea about that but it might need your help."

"Whatever help you need, you will get."

Chapter 34

The dogs were barking as they pulled into the farmyard, Hendrik's truck was parked by the steps and both he and Johann were sitting on the stoop, beers in hand.

"Ah, the walking wounded." Said Hendrik as Martin walked up the steps.

"You need to be more careful around firearms, my friend."

"Don't I know it, I'll be quite happy if I never see another gun as long as I live, I have seen death and destruction through guns too often in the past few months."

"How so?"

"I found Jo due to it, the Doctor who came to pick us up was shot whilst sitting next to Jo in the vehicle that we were in. I was threatened with a gun twice in that same truck and was forced to kill twice in order for us to survive. And now this little incident. So yes, I have had my fill of guns."

Hendrik looked at Martin, then Jo.

"Is this true," he asked Jo, "they shot the Doctor sitting next to you and threatened Martin?"

"Yes!"

A shadow passed through Jo's eyes and an involuntary shiver raced through her body.

"Dr Tom." she murmured, remembering the event.

Looking Hendrik in the eye she said,

"Every word. Other things also happened that I do not wish to talk about but without Martin I would not be here."

Hendrik looked at his feet, raising his head he looked at Martin.

"Sorry, I didn't mean to offend."

"No offence taken."

"Johann I must go, I have work to do. Thanks for the beer. Johanna, Martin good day to you."

Anika appeared from the house,

"Hendrik's a good man, he meant no offence."

"That's OK, none taken. I just thought it best to put the record straight."

"He is going to arrange for workmen to repair the damage, so he will be coming back with men and materials, probably tomorrow."

"If he needs help, I'm willing and able, well willing at least."

"Thank you Martin but maybe you need to rest."

"Sit here with Johann. I'll get you a beer. Johanna, come, we have food to prepare."

Anika and Jo made a light supper. It was late in the evening, a large meal would have been too much to sleep on.

A curtain had been nailed to the wall in the remains of Jo's parents' bedroom doorway to give them some privacy.

Morning came and Martin woke with a throbbing headache. Sitting up in bed, he felt slightly nauseous but it passed, showering without getting his head wet was difficult though.

Breakfast and Jo were waiting for him in the kitchen.

"I'm coming with you," she said, "I don't want to risk you falling ill out there."

"Thanks, that's one worry off my mind."

Having fed and watered the sheep, they sat side by side on a rocky outcrop enjoying the beauty and serenity of the landscape.

"Earlier, in the kitchen you said, 'That's one worry off my mind', what did you mean?"

"I'm worried about you, your Pa and what will happen if my ear doesn't heal before my visa runs out. Outwardly you appear to be coping but I'm worried that what I told you yesterday might have upset you. Your Pa must have suffered a problem, to act the way he did yesterday. I think some of it may be down to frustration and as I said, I have a plan in mind for that. As for the visa, only time will tell."

"I'm fine, in case you hadn't noticed. I haven't had one of those dreams for a while. I will admit that what you told me was surprising but not perhaps unexpected."

They sat in silence for a while.

"Martin, will you tell me everything?"

"Pardon?"

"Tell me everything that happened from that day in the village."

"You know most of it."

"Yes but not all and I want to know everything now. I don't want to have snippets of information coming back to me."

"I don't think that would be a good idea, maybe we should ask Dr Dhal."

"To hell with Dr Dhal!"

Jo was getting angry.

"I want to know, now."

Martin could sense that there would be no way of placating Jo.

He thought for a while.

"OK, I will tell you the whole story but in the presence of your parents and only if they agree to it. If what I tell you causes you harm, you may need some help that only they can give."

"OK but I think Ma only, Pa is too ill."

"Agreed."

Sitting in an armchair opposite Jo and Anika with a pot of hot coffee on the table between them, Martin began. Starting from the arrival of the militia into the village, he narrated in detail all that happened, closely watching Jo for signs of distress. Anika held Jo's hand the whole time, gently squeezing it in affection as some of the details took their toll, questioning Martin occasionally for clarification on certain statements.

Jo sat in silence, only her eyes and body movements betraying her signs of anxiety.

Finally reaching the point when Jo was airlifted to South Africa, Martin relaxed and sat back in the chair. He reached for the coffee, it was cold but he drank it anyway.

Jo and Anika stared at him for a while until Jo, tears in her eyes, turned to her Ma.

Anika letting go of Jo's hand, pulled her close and hugged her until the tears stopped flowing.

Releasing Jo from her embrace, Anika reached over the table and took Martin's hands.

"Thank you. Johann told me some of that after you had spoken with him but not all, I guess he tried to spare me some of the more, shall we say, distasteful details."

"Oh Martin, how can I ever thank you. You put yourself in danger to save a stranger and not just once."

"It may sound strange but I feel as if a weight has been lifted from my shoulders. I can look forward to life without worrying that something dark will come back to haunt me."

"Hopefully! Would you like me to tell your Ma about what happened in Cape Town?"

"Martin! How could you?"

"It's OK Johanna, I know, said Anika, I saw it when you came back that evening. The way you glowed, like you used too when you achieved a goal you had set yourself and the way your cheeks flushed with guilt when you saw me. Yes, the Johanna, of old had returned, unfortunately Pa's accident took away the moment."

"Pardon me ladies, am I missing something?"

They looked at him, a knowing glint in their eyes.

"I don't know what you are intimating. I was talking about the event that led to going into Margarette's shop."

"Oh!" Exclaimed Jo, before bursting into laughter. "Yes, tell Ma."

Before Martin could continue, they heard the sound of a truck turning into the farmyard and the sound of several voices and equipment being unloaded.

Hendrik appeared at the door.

"Ah, Mevrou Anika, I have men and materials to repair you home, will I be able to start now?"

"Come in Hendrik, yes of course, I will get Johann into another room and then move the furniture."

"I have men to move whatever is needed, if you look after Johann, we will do the rest."

He turned and barked orders to several Africans who were standing beside his truck.

Johann decided that he would sit on the stoep. Hendrik organised his men then alternated between supervising them and talking to Johann. By sundown, the work was completed.

Apart from driving out with Jo to feed and check on the sheep, Martin spent the afternoon in Johann's workshop only coming out to talk to Hendrik just as he was leaving.

Later that evening as they sat relaxing on the stop, Martin asked Anika if she had a seamstress's tape measure.

"Why yes, of course, would you like me to get it for you now?"

"No, but can you measure around Johann's head, like you would for sizing a hat, over the bandage of course."

"May I ask why?"

"Yes Martin, why?" Asked Jo.

"I need to buy a motorcycle helmet for Johann and it must fit over his head now. Pieter will come over tomorrow and take me to town to buy one."

"Why Pieter? I can take you."

"I asked Hendrik where I could buy one and then he said that given my damaged head and hearing, he would send Pieter to drive me. How could I refuse?"

"Hmm, OK but why does Pa need a helmet?"

"All will be revealed tomorrow."

Chapter 35

Pieter arrived in the Mercedes.

"Pa needs the truck." he said.

"He said you need a motorcycle helmet for Menheer but maybe it's for you?"

"He's right. It's for Johann, although he doesn't know it yet."

As they sped down the road to Willowmore, Jo once again became the topic of conversation.

"Have I upset Johanna?"

"Not at all, if you are referring to the other night when I nearly blew my head off, I don't think she meant to be sharp with you, she was just a little stressed, as we all probably were."

"Oh, that's good."

"She likes you a lot."

"Really?"

"Yes, really. She has told me of your exploits together in your younger days and how she enjoys your company."

The shop assistant was bewildered. Martin wanted to buy a helmet for someone with a bandaged head when he himself had a bandaged head.

"Sir, a helmet must be a tight fit on the person's head and if that person has a damaged head, then he should not ride a motorcycle. Also, I would like to point out that when the bandage is removed from the person's head, the helmet will be useless, it will be too loose."

"Yes, I know. Thank you."

Helmet in a plastic bag, they left the shop and headed home.

"Martin. If I may be so bold, why does Menheer need a helmet?"

"I have made a modification to one of the quads, to allow Johann to come out with us when we feed the sheep but as his head is not yet healed and he is a little unsteady I thought a helmet would be advisable. I just hope it fits. Come on, if we get a move on, we can try it this afternoon."

Jo came to meet them as they drove into the farmyard. She looked coyly at Pieter but when he smiled at her, she immediately smiled back.

"Ooh, is that for me." Jo asked Martin, spying the bag.

"No, it's for your Pa, as if you didn't know."

She feigned disappointment for a few seconds, then laughed.

"Are you ready to feed the sheep?" Martin asked her.

"Ready and waiting."

"Right, see if you can get your Pa to wear this, Pieter and I will get the quads."

"Pardon?"

"Don't question, just do." Martin said haughtily, as he handed over the bag, a smile on his face.

"Yes Boss." said Jo tugging a forelock as she took the bag.

Pieter just looked in amazement at the two of them.

Driving into the farmyard on the quads, they found Jo and Anika holding a helmeted Johann by each arm.

Martin pulled close to them, switched off the quad and dismounted.

"Right Johann, let's get you on this contraption, shall we?"

Martin had adapted and fitted a seat back with safety strap to one of the quads so that Johann could ride as a passenger and be safely strapped on.

With Johann in place, Martin asked Jo to take the driver's position, her Pa could hold on to her waist for more support if needed.

Martin and Pieter would ride the other quad.

"OK Johann, shall we check on your sheep?"

Johann's face was a picture of pure joy.

"Jo, you go ahead and drive slowly, we'll follow. Any problems just stop."

"Anika, do you think the dogs would like to come along?"

As they started along the track Max and Samson came bounding up, running on either side of their master.

On returning, Johann was eased off the quad, he stood holding onto the load rack whilst Jo eased off his helmet.

A broad smile broke across his face.

Addressing Jo and Martin he said,

"You should have done that sooner, beats sitting in that chair any day."

Jo and Anika helped him to 'that' chair on the stoep and placed a cold beer in his hand.

Jo ambushed Pieter as he returned to his car. Martin saw them talking and then embrace for a few seconds before he got into the car. As he drove out of the farmyard, Jo waved to him.

Johann noticed it also.

As the days passed Johann's demeanour changed, he was gradually reverting to his old self. In the mornings instead of lying in bed, he was up and ready, motorcycle helmet in his hand impatiently waiting for Jo and Martin to bring the quad into the farmyard so he could go with them to the sheep.

He was becoming more active physically but his memory still failed on occasions and that caused him concern.

"It's OK Pa," said Jo, "it takes time for the brain to heal but you will get there, don't worry."

Returning from his check-up at the hospital where they had decided that his wound had healed enough for the bandages to be dispensed with, Johann instructed Anika to make him a soft head covering that he could wear under his helmet.

"This helmet is too big now," he complained. "My head will rattle around like a pea in a drum."

Anika fashioned him what looked like an aircrew helmet of old, only made of blanket material rather than leather and lined it with cotton cloth.

"I hope it won't make me too hot." Was his retort when Anika offered it to him.

"Well, if you don't like it, you can always buy a smaller helmet." She replied.

"Ah, I'm sure it will be fine." he said as he tried it on.

"That looks great Pa, now try the helmet over the top. There, it fits perfectly."

The days turned to weeks; Martin had to make a decision.

His visa was running out, it was possible to extend it but did he need to?

His ear wound had healed but his hearing was still impaired. He decided to visit the local doctor.

"Yes Mr Newman, your eardrum is healing nicely, no need to worry about getting it wet any more. Your hearing will probably return to its normal level over time. You will just have to be patient."

"But what about flying?"

"No problem there either, although it wouldn't hurt to use an earplug, you know the type they use when out shooting."

Decision Time! Johann was almost back to his former self, he didn't need Martin's help.

Jo was spending more and more time with Pieter, in fact apart from when working on the farm and meal times, Martin hardly saw her.

Returning with Johann from tending the sheep the following morning, Martin was pleased to find that Jo had gone with Pieter to Willowmore and might be some time. He called the airline.

Yes, seats were available that afternoon.

He sat at the bedside table and wrote what was possibly the hardest letter of his life, then sealed it in an envelope.

Having packed his trusty rucksack, he walked into the kitchen where Johann and Anika were sitting at the table drinking coffee.

Seeing him with his rucksack, Johann stood and said,

"I wondered when this would happen, you don't have to go, you know that, don't you?"

"Yes. I came here, to South Africa, to satisfy myself that the promise that I made, to make sure that Jo arrived home safe and well, was fulfilled. I think that is the case. But more than that, I have been welcomed into your and her home and have, I hope, made good friends with you all. I could not have wished for a warmer welcome."

"I don't like goodbyes. This is actually quite hard for me to do but I feel that now is the time."

Anika, initially stunned by Martin's impending departure walked over and grasped his hands in hers, looking him full in the eyes she said.

"Martin, you are more than a friend, you have become one of the family and will always be welcome in this house."

"Thank you, that means a lot to me."

"Jo is a beautiful, attractive and clever young woman and it is fair to say that I love her dearly but in a completely platonic way, as a close and much cherished friend.

It has been my pleasure to know her, to see her change from that broken, traumatised body that I found in the hut to the happy, almost carefree, person that she is now.

That is why I must leave now, whilst she is away. Cowardly, perhaps, but I think the least painful."

"I have one small favour to ask of you."

"Of course."

"I have written this letter to Jo. Please give it to her when she returns."

As Martin drove out of the farmyard and down the track, Johann and Anika stood side by side holding hands and waving.

Chapter 36

"Where's Martin??" Asked Jo as she carried in an armful of groceries, "We could do with some help."

"He's gone." Answered her Pa.

"Gone, gone where?"

"To the airport, he's going home."

"No, no, he can't, we need him. I need him!"

"He left you a letter, Ma has it."

Anika gave her the letter. Jo tore it open immediately.

Dearest Jo,

This is probably the hardest letter I have ever had to write.

The time has come for me to return home.

When I found you in that hut all those months ago, traumatised, battered and left to die, I made a promise to myself to get you to safety and medical attention. Seeing you like that really tugged at my heartstrings.

Despite all the setbacks that we encountered on that journey, I thought that having gotten you to the Uni-Med facility my promise was fulfilled, you cannot imagine the anger and frustration I felt on finding that they had shipped you out without even letting me say goodbye and then refusing to even tell me where you had gone.

If it had not been for Dr Max, I probably would still be wondering about you. It was his idea to write a letter to you and send it to your head office.

I gave it a couple of weeks and then checked my emails every day for a reply, I thought that even if you couldn't reply, someone might do so on your behalf.

As the weeks turned into months, I had almost given up hope, the lack of it ate away at me.

Oh how my heart sang when I saw your email, I couldn't wait to see you again.

The rest, of course, you know.

To say that I'm love with you would be an understatement but it is not as a lover, it is more perhaps how a father would love a daughter; a daughter which, unfortunately due to the cruelty of nature, I cannot have.

I wish you only the best that life can offer. You have gone through so much pain and anguish since I have known you and yet managed to come out smiling, you deserve nothing less.

Martin.

"Oh Ma, he's really gone. When did he leave?"

"About one hour ago."

"Where to?"

"Well, he arrived through Port Elizabeth. I guess he'll go the same way." Said Johann.

"Pieter, get in the car we are going after him."

"But he's been gone an hour, we'll never catch him."

"Pieter, I'm going! With or without you."

"Okay, okay."

Pieter drove well above the speed limits.

"I hope there's no radar, Pa will kill me if I get a fine."

As Pieter pulled up at the car park barrier, Jo jumped out.

"Park up and come and find me, I'll be in departures."

She raced to the terminal.

A security guard was diligently searching everyone entering the terminal, as Jo stood in the line, she visually scanned the terminal for Martin.

At last, inside, but where was he, was she too late?

No, he was queuing at departure control.

"Martin," she shouted. No response. She shouted louder. "Martin!"

He turned and made his way out of the queue, several people turned to watch.

Jo flew at him, hugging him tightly. Tears of joy flowing down her cheeks.

"Martin, you can't go. You must stay. I need you to stay."

He looked at her tear-stained face, brushed away the still flowing tears from her cheeks and said,

"I have to go. You have a new life to lead, we had our adventure but now your time has come to move on."

He spied Pieter coming towards them.

"Pieter loves you dearly, almost as much as I do but in a different way. You two are made for each other. You are young and beautiful and have so much to offer, not just to each other but to all who know you. You told me that you wanted to help people, remember, like Margarette. Do it, I know you can."

The public address system called Martin's flight.

"Look after her, Pieter or you'll have me to answer to. I know where there's a shotgun," he said, touching his ear and grinning.

"Yes Sir. I will."

"Now take her home and drive carefully."

"I will."

Prising himself from the still sobbing Jo, he handed her to Pieter, stealing a kiss on her cheek before he did so, then headed back to the departure control desk.

He didn't look back; he dare not because Jo would have seen the tears streaming down his face.